THE CHANGEUP

NICOLE FALLS

Silent N Publishing

Acknowledgments

shake: a simple question spiraled into an entire plot. thank you for your big brain, pal.

jilly: thank you for helping me get settled in the end.

c&j&s: for the safest of spaces with the biggest of laughs. xo!

twc: accountability is key, amirite?

FIRST INNING

"You ready, lil girl?" a gravelly voice asked me, seeping into my bedroom.

I rolled my eyes at my father still referring to me as a little girl despite me being well beyond the age of girlhood.

"Almost, daddy," I called back, grabbing one of my dad caps to complete my no muss no fuss aesthetic.

I was outfitted in what was my uniform of sorts on most summer days, denim cutoffs with a lightweight flannel shirt tied around my waist, a V-neck white tee, and a dad cap perched backwards atop my long messy hair that I barely bothered to straighten. I was lucky that the bed head look managed to be somewhat appealing thanks to the 3B curl pattern I'd been told that inherited from my mother. A fanny pack – with all of my money, identification and other essentials – slung around my shoulders completed the look. A carefully curated façade of minimalist care that took me at least forty-five minutes to perfect before I darkened my doorway.

"Geffri Denise Robinson if you don't hurry up," my father called out again and I had to laugh at his impatience.

We were headed out to a ballgame and that old man hated walking in at the start of the game. Ever since we had attended games together when I was a little girl, he'd have me at the gates as soon as they opened, so we could get to his season ticket holder seats and bask in the beauty of the ballpark before it was sullied with the players of the game. When it came to baseball, my father was a bit obsessive. He was never quite a stats guy, but he loved the purity of the game – few technicalities that precluded complications with scoring. The rules of the game were cut and dry, with little room for ambiguity, just as he liked it.

"I'm coming, Daddy! Hold your horses," I yelled back, giggling under my breath again because I knew he was downstairs stewing.

I looked over to the clock to see that we had more than enough time for us to actually make it to the ballpark within his allotted sit and settle time. Since I lived within walking distance, we were going to hoof it over to the stadium to watch our local squad try to snap a four-game losing streak. Growing up, our local team hadn't ever been the one to root for especially, they were a middling team at best, but the quality time that I spent with my dad out at the field was irreplaceable. Instead of getting his pressure up even further, I jogged out of my room, down the stairs and greeted him where he stood beside the front door harrumphing and checking his watch.

"Okay, Pops, let's roll," I said, opening the door and gesturing for him to precede me.

A quick shake of his head and furrowed brow let me know that I needed to exit first, despite being the one who would lock up. So, I sauntered through the door and then waited at just beyond the door's threshold for him to step through and shut the door. A quick entry of my passcode for the electronic lock and then we were off, down the sidewalk, joining the throngs of folks who were milling through my neighborhood to eventually land at the ballpark. It was a gorgeous Saturday afternoon. One that, if I didn't have plans with Pops, would have definitely seen me out in the streets brunching with my girls and day drinking on someone's rooftop. But, as was our custom, every Saturday home game he and I had a standing date at the ballpark. Well, that was if I wasn't away in some capacity. Pops' fervor for baseball had easily been passed down to me since I was essentially his little shadow as a young pup. Gramma Robinson hated that I would pass over hanging out with her and doing all manner of girly things in order to either trail behind my dad and soak up whatever he was doing or run around her neighborhood with the crew of young boys who lived on her block. She'd send me outside with my hair in two perfect plaits and a cute little dress and I'd come back inside after a few hours looking like Pig Pen from Charlie Brown.

The walk over to the ballpark took a bit longer than anticipated since Pops couldn't move as swiftly as he used to. He hated when I brought that up and insisted that he wasn't missing a beat, but I couldn't help but worry about him. He and my mother were older in life when me – their surprise miracle baby – had appeared. Mommy had been pregnant four times before me and lost the child at various stages of gestation. She and Pops had just about given up on having any children of their own when I was conceived. The pregnancy was a rough one for Mommy and ultimately culminated in her untimely demise. So, Pops had been my sole caretaker from birth – with help from his family and friends – and he filled the roles of mom and dad fairly well. I didn't have much contact with my mother's side of the family – many of them were displaced that she had carried me to full-term once she was told the complicated risks on her life that delivery could bring. This was all secondhand information I'd learned from snooping and eavesdropping on grown folks' conversations over the years. I'd never asked Pops about it directly and it wasn't something he'd readily shared.

"Are you listening to me, lil girl?" my dad's voice broke into my thoughts.

I turned to him with a grin that usually got me out of whatever trouble I was in with him since I was a little girl.

"Sorry, Pops, you're gonna have to speak into my good ear," I giggled, moving to the other side of the sidewalk and tuning into what he had been going on about.

"I said," he repeated himself, annoyance clear in his tone, "are you giving any more thought to that tryout information that I sent you."

I sighed harshly, trying not to roll my eyes, "I actually haven't, Pops. I don't know if there will be any scheduling conflicts."

"Okay, I won't press you, Geff, but I just…wish you'd consider giving it a go. Even if it's just for your old man."

I sidled up closer to him, throwing an arm over his shoulder as we strolled, "Really, Pops? I thought you were above emotional manipulation…"

"I just don't want to sit back and watch you let this opportunity pass you by. Whatever happened to the little girl who was going to be the first female pitcher in Major League Baseball?"

"She went to undergrad and pitched for a Division II school with a group of young men who completely ruined the game for her going forward is what happened, Pops!"

"Point taken, but you also saw that this is the women's national team, right?"

I chuckled, shaking my head, "I'm out of practice, Pops."

"Oh…somebody else coaching that softball team down there at Jones High or is that you?"

I sighed again, "Pops!"

He held up his hands in surrender, "Fine…*fine*, I won't press you. But…I just want you to give it some serious consideration."

"I am, Pops," I murmured, "trust me, you just don't know how much."

Soon we were at the ballpark, so I shook my head to clear it of any lingering thoughts of the things we'd discussed on our walk and pointed my mind toward enjoying the game and this time with Pops. To say I was a daddy's girl would be a gross understatement. Pops was *The Man* ™ in my eyes, few could match up or compare. He was the first person I confided any of my secrets in, the only one who knew everything about me there was to know – even the parts I tried to keep buried deep beneath the surface.

Three innings in and Pops sent me to fetch his one beer that he was allowed to have for the game. I gave him grief initially before consenting and climbing over the empty rows of seats behind us to head to a beer vendor. Pops hated drinking canned or bottled beers, so he always went inside to concessions and got whatever was on tap – usually a big-name light beer. In the years since I'd grown up coming to this park with him – and eventually being able to imbibe beer and spirits legally – the park had come a long way with the offerings available for those who liked an alcoholic beverage. I was barely out of our section when my body collided with what felt like a brick wall and knocked me flat on my ass. I looked up to see a massive wall of a man, with an apologetic look on his face as he extended a hand to help me up.

"My bad, youngin', I didn't see you there," the man crooned, keeping his hands in mine until I was fully upright.

"Babe, that's why I told you and Noah to stop acting like kids horsing around," a soft female voice called out from behind the man, "I'm so sorry, sweetheart. Nathan, did you apologize to this girl?"

"He did, Miss," I said, biting back a smile at her clear chastisement of two very grown men.

"I didn't hear it, Nathan. You know what…actually – why don't you and Noah go to our seats, y'all have done enough damage and give me your wallet. I'm gonna treat this young lady to whatever she wants at concessions. What's your name, sweetheart?"

"Geffri," I replied.

"Geffri and I are about to buy the bar with your card, Nathan. What shall I bring you back?"

"Oh no, you're good, I wasn't really paying attention to where I was going either," I said quickly, trying to extricate myself from this awkward situation.

"Excuse me, miss lady?" I heard a voice ask over my shoulder, "I think you dropped this?"

A long caramel brown arm held my dad cap in my direction. I hadn't even realized that my little tumble had knocked it off my head. I grabbed it gingerly from the person, letting my eyes slowly trail up the arm to the face of a very handsome man.

"Y-yes, thank you," I said, placing the hat back atop my head, facing in the right direction this time to hide my face a bit.

I felt my face growing hot and knew the redness was spreading all over my cheeks at the simple brushing of fingers between me and the man. Nathan and his wife, whose name I hadn't caught in their back and forth, were still going back and forth so I discreetly moved around him as I continued on my way to the beer stand. I heard Nathan's wife calling after me, but I just hotfooted my way forward, not wanting to get sucked into whatever was going on between those two. I found my dad's favorite beer guy, Sam, grabbed us two drafts, tipped Sam way more than necessary, and picked my way back to my seat. Since I was holding the two beers, I had to scooch past Pops to get back to my seat upon my return.

"Took ya long enough, lil girl. I liked to die of heatstroke out here without a cool beverage," Pops joked, winking at me as I handed him his beer and retook my seat.

"Hush up old man!" I grinned back at him.

"You get lost on the way to Sam?"

"No! Look, you got ya beer, man. Let's just enjoy the rest of this game."

"Fine, fine!" Pops chuckled and turned his attention back toward the field.

We enjoyed friendly heckling of the players and lamenting with our seat neighbors about the poor performance being put on by our squad for a couple innings before the unimaginable happened. The ballpark has all of these little interstitial time-wasting activities that they trot out during television commercial breaks and between innings. Normally it's children competing in silly contests, but today they did a random draw of seats and gathered a handful of patrons to compete in a pitching contest. I swear if I was able to prove it, I would have thought my father set me up, but the fact that he was just as surprised as I was when the camera man zoomed in on my face as one of the folks who would be participating in this contest gave me pause. Pops wasn't very good at feigning emotions, so I knew it was a random luck of the draw more than anything else, but that didn't stop the nerves that built.

Despite playing the sport for more than half of my life, I was out of practice. I'd put down my glove after my time playing in undergrad, which put me a smooth four years out of practice. I did, every now and again, get a good workout with my arm as I coached our varsity softball team, but that style of pitching was very different from an actual baseball pitch. Still, I strode over to the section on the field where they were corralling us to line up for our shot on the mound. There were four of us, two men and two women, in this contest. My fellow competitors were in varying stages of physical fitness. The first of the two men was a white guy who looked to be in his mid to late forties with a paunch the size of Santa's and male pattern baldness that called to mind Kevin from The Office. The other man was a tall, thin white guy with platinum blonde hair and piercing blue eyes who looked like the number one to the other guy's zero shaped body composition. The other woman, I couldn't tell if she was Latina or of some other ethnicity, but I'd be damned if I wasn't somewhat intimidated by her brolic stance.

The on-field correspondent was this cute little sista who looked to be around my age with copper toned skin that looked like it'd been brushed with *Fenty Beauty Body Lava*, a large afro puff atop her head, and legs for days. She introduced herself to us quickly before we'd be broadcast on the jumbo screen and ran down the rules of the game. We were expected to throw a pitch from the mound to a faux catcher and the pitch radar would be tracking our speed. Whoever threw the fastest pitch would be invited back out to the ballpark to enjoy the game from a luxury suite and also throw out the first pitch as a hometown hero at whichever game they chose to come back to attend. I knew Pops would gag over me winning, so I was charged up and ready to let one fly. The tall, thin, white guy was talking mad trash as we waited to be marched onto the mound, telling the rest of us how he'd been the best pitcher at his high school, and we should all just pack it up. The big guy seemed to be tuning him out while the lady looked like she was half a second from ripping his head off and lobbing it as her pitch. Dude looked a smooth twenty years removed from high school if those crow's feet around his eyes told the real story, so I wasn't sweating him too hard.

We drew straws to figure out our pecking order and I'd be going last. Fred – the big guy was first, then Griselda, then Sven, and finally me. We marched out to the center of the field and the correspondent, Gina, announced us all to the crowd. I peered toward the section where Pops was sitting and saw him standing with a grin a mile wide when my name was announced. After Gina got the crowd to cheer for all of us, the contest began. We would be given two throws each in the first round. Those would be averaged and then the two of us with the highest cumulative speeds would compete head to head with one final pitch each to determine the winner. Sven was still talking shit when Fred stepped up to take his turn and Griselda finally snapped at him.

"For the love of all things holy, will you shut up, man?" she gritted out, "We get it. You led your high school baseball team to victory when you pitched a no hitter thirty-two years ago. That's not today though, my guy."

Sven sputtered before retorting that he'd only been out of high school for ten years and I tried to hide the surprise on my face. Those ten years that passed must've been rough because homeboy looked old enough to have taught me in high school. I tuned them out in favor of flexing my fingers one by one before grabbing a ball from the bucket of balls we were expected to choose to throw from. A comforting sense of familiarity rushed through me as I ran my fingers over the red yarn that held the cowhide that made up the outside of the ball together. As was my tradition before warming up to play as a kid, I flitted my fingers over each stitch, unconsciously counting all one hundred and eight of them.

"Geffri...you ready?" the mistress of ceremonies, Gina called out to me.

I was so zoned out that I didn't even realize that those other two had gone before me. I nodded, moving toward the center of the mound, awaiting the signal from our catcher. At his nod, I rolled my shoulders, getting into the position, wound up, and let one fly. When it left my hand, it felt awkward and seeing that it was way beyond the strike zone made sense as to why that was. But it must've had some fire to it since I saw the catcher shaking his hand in the mitt before getting back into position. I looked to my left at the jumbotron to see the first pitch's speed.

"Whew! Geffri came to give the competition some heat. Seventy-nine, out the gate with no warmup? Sheesh." Gina gushed, turning to my competitors and cajoling them good naturedly, "Y'all might wanna pack it up, guys."

That comment made me briefly glance up at the screen to see the other folks' speeds that were displayed on the screen. Fred had pitched thirty-five and thirty-seven mile per hour attempts. Griselda brought the heat a bit more than Fred with sixty and sixty-three mile per hour pitches. Looking at his speeds, I'd wondered if Sven was short for Svengali with the way he'd been trying to convince us of his prolific arm that was just barely better than Griselda's, with pitches at sixty-five and sixty-seven. I rolled my shoulders once more, squared my stance and then threw my second pitch. I adjusted my grip slightly, throwing a curveball this time instead of the two-seam fastball I'd chucked my first time out. That one clocked in a seventy-seven, clearly cementing my first-place status to move forward into the next round. Gina excused Griselda and Fred quickly with nominal gift cards to the club store and turned to Sven and me.

"All right, you two. Y'all ready to see who's gonna win this grand prize?"

I nodded, grinning a bit as Sven said, "Yep, looking forward to sending this little girl home packing. I was holding back in the first round because I didn't want to embarrass anyone, but now all bets are off."

Gina had a look on her face that clearly screamed a dismissive "*um okay, sis*" and it took everything in me not to react externally. She announced that we would keep our same pitching order, so Sven was up first. He took his time settling atop the mound with a cocky swagger that was reminiscent of so many boys from my past. I knew before he even grabbed a ball from the bucket, that he was about to damn near throw his back out trying to out throw me and I bit back a giggle at the thought of it. And just like those fools left behind in the years in which I'd been playing this game, I knew he'd ultimately end up embarrassing himself. Instead of succumbing to the stupid, threatened male ego energy he was putting off, I turned to find Pops in the crowd. I looked in the general direction of the section that our season tickets were in, trying to make eye contact with him. I'd just focused my gaze on him when Gina nudged me, indicating that it was my turn to give it a go. I didn't even bother looking to see what speed Sven was able to hit on his most recent attempt, instead just channeling my energy into throwing a heater of a four-seam fastball.

Once the ball left my fingers, it just felt good. I remembered how much I'd loved being in the thick of playing the game, holding the balance of the other team's fate in my hands. I got off on being able to lull guys into unsuspecting victims when I was on the mound. No matter how much buzz was generated with the novelty of me being the only girl on most of the teams I played on, I was consistently underestimated. I came to learn that most people thought I was a fluke or…some sort of mascot for the teams on which I played, a visual representation of equity but no one to really give serious consideration. Time and time again, I proved folks wrong and today's exhibition against Sven would be no different. When I looked over to the screen that displayed the speed of the ball I'd just let go, even I was impressed. It was on the higher end of my most impressive speeds, clocking in at eighty-seven miles per hour. Just one measly mile off of my personal best. The crowd went up in a roar of a cheer, which was when my eyes shifted to see what Sven's pitch had been. Seventy-five miles per hour was where he'd topped out. I smirked and offered a hand for him to shake in a show of sportsmanship. He sneered in my direction, ignoring my hand and stalking off the field. I looked over to Gina who just shrugged as she led me off the field and into an office where she hooked me up with all of the information that I'd need to set up collecting my prize.

Making my way back to my seat, I was stopped by entirely too many strangers who wanted to offer words of congrats or ask if I was a ringer planed by the ballpark. I shook off the latter of those who approached me with stupid energy, politely brushing them off with the insistence that I needed to get back to my father. By the time I reached Pops again, he was sitting there with his chest puffed out, bragging on me to the folks who were sitting behind us, saying he taught me everything I knew. Which was the truth, Pops had been somewhat of a legend in his high school days, but instead of accepting a scholarship to a university to play ball and possibly move forward to the major leagues, he decided to take a job in a local factory instead – to help his mother be able to provide for his younger siblings since their father had skated off the scene with some young hoe, leaving my grandma to fend for herself. Pops said he never regretted his decision to help his family, but I could definitely tell that part of my success in baseball felt like a way for him to fulfill dreams that'd been unfairly truncated, in my opinion anyway. As an only child, I didn't really *understand* his decision, but I definitely respected it above all.

I tried slinking past him to little fanfare, but he definitely led our section in a reprisal of the cheering that the entire crowd had done at the conclusion of the contest. I waved them off, shaking my head with a grin. I lifted a hand in thanks before collapsing into my seat next to Pops. He leaned my way, stretching an arm behind me to pull me in for a hug and a kiss to my temple.

"Proud of you, Speedy," he rumbled, and I grinned at his usage of my childhood nickname.

"Thanks, Pops," I replied.

The rest of the game passed without incident, and our guys managed a win, which made the stroll back to my place pleasurable. Pops left as soon as we got back to my place, but not before reminding me to go see my grandmother tomorrow since it was her birthday. That was hardly a reminder he needed to give me since I ended up at her house nearly every Sunday anyway. She still made an old school soul food dinner every week with enough food to feed the damned neighborhood despite having lived alone for more than twenty years at this point.

SECOND INNING

"Oh shit...P, we have a celebrity in our midst. Miss Robinson, can we please have your autograph?" Blair gushed as I crossed the threshold of the door that she held open letting me into her place.

I rolled my eyes as I strolled in and gave her a quick side hug as I made my way to the living room where our other friend Parker sat giggling. I gave Parker a quick hug before sliding down next to her on the sofa.

"Hey superstar," Parker crooned.

I should have known to expect this from the two of them. We'd all met the summer before our first year of undergrad. We were all on campus as a part of a collegiate athletic orientation type deal and ended up being placed together in a triple – a configuration we found ourselves in for the entirety of our undergraduate careers. We clicked instantly, which for me was something a little different since I hadn't had many friends growing up. I was always a bit of a loner, too in my head to really make friends easily. I'd always managed a bit of cordiality with teammates and classmates. I'd gotten better as I got older, but never had any real deal, true blue friends until Blair and Parker came along. These two brought me out of my shell and made me feel loved and supported in ways that I'd never experienced outside of my dad and grandparents. They got on my nerves more than a little bit, but we were stuck together for the rest of eternity, a bond for which I was truly thankful.

"Here y'all go," I groaned, slumping forward to rest my elbows on knees.

"It's not every day that one of your best friends blows up on the internet and goes viral," Parker reasoned.

I groaned again, "I shoulda never agreed to even participate in that stupid contest."

It took less than eight hours after the conclusion of the game for someone to submit a video of the pitching contest between Sven and I to Bleacher Report. It was calling him out for damn near throwing his entire body onto the ground trying to beat me – a *#SCNotTop10* moment in the making, for sure. But then the extended version of the clip somehow got uploaded and the narrative shifted from the idiocy of his move to who in the hell was I and whether or not I was a ringer, and this was a stunt by the ballpark. From there, someone who knew of me must've recognized because I then went on to be tagged a bajillion different times by folks sharing the video and varying levels of commentary. It was amusing at first, but damn near a week in it was now just annoying. My Twitter mentions were filled with way too many trolls talking shit. I'd ignored them all for the most part but there was one who got under my skin a little too deeply.

Noah Fence. An ironic, coincidental name of a man who had done nothing but work to offend me over and over. Damn near a week later, and his johnny come lately ass decided to chime in with his shitty viewpoint. He was a sports blogger, creator of a website called *brothas&bats*, which was a

Major League Baseball centric blog, but he also freelanced for a couple of larger sports outlets. It started simply enough, he'd retweeted the B/R tweet saying that he could still hit one off me, no matter how fast the faulty pitch gun said I'd thrown. I paid him as much dust as I did the rest of the trolls until someone thought it prudent to tag me in a thread where he'd gone on a tirade about how too much was being made of a fluke of a performance. The person who tagged me meant well, if their reply was any indication as they'd attached some film from my undergrad days of proof that I wasn't a one trick pony. I didn't, however, appreciate still being dragged into the narrative as they continued to argue back and forth with this Noah character. Especially when it veered off into the territory of questioning my abilities.

As my phone pinged with yet another notification from Twitter with his handle in it, I'd finally had enough and replied.

@noahhhfence312: @moundsandhounds i appreciate your fervor for ya girl @notthegiraffe8, but i remain unimpressed. *shrug* i bet i could hit at least a double off her, easy.

@moundsandhounds: @noahhhfence312 you're tripping, dude! A former high school star isn't hitting anything off of @notthegiraffe8.

@noahhhfence312: @moundsandhounds @notthegiraffe8 **collegiate star. put some respeck on my career before injury. i raked for a solid two years at the university level, fam.

@noahhhfence312: @moundsandhounds @notthegiraffe8 i'm going yard off any pitch your girl would send my way, trust me. i know how to use my bat.

@notthegiraffe8: @noahhhfence312 @moundsandhounds Ironic that you're asking for respect when fully disrespecting me right in my mentions. Oh…and you couldn't even hit a ball I set on a tee for you…*fam*.

@noahhhfence312: @notthegiraffe8 no disrespect intended, sweetheart, just stating my opinion is all.

@notthegiraffe8: @noahhhfence312 So you do know how to remove someone who isn't the intended target of your tweets from the narrative? Great. Next time you'd do well to remember keeping my name out your mouth as well. And I'm not your sweetheart.

@noahhhfence312: noted, @notthegiraffe8. you don't want this smoke tho. you know i'd embarrass you out there.

@notthegiraffe8: @noahhhfence312 Smoke? Please. I don't play with other people's children.

@noahhhfence312: @notthegiraffe8 oh trust me, i ain't playing. i'm very serious. whaddya say? let me show you what I'm workin' with and let the public see if your little pitching sideshow was a fluke.

@notthegiraffe8: @noahhhfence312 You're not worth the time nor energy.

"So, you seriously asked for us to get together today because you had news, came into my house and proceeded to ignore us, woooooow," Blair crowed, "the claudacity."

Parker and I both broke down into laughter over her usage of "claudacity", a call back to an idiot in undergrad who'd used that non-word repeatedly in a presentation in one of our lower level current events courses when he'd meant audacity. We'd adopted it into our lexicon immediately, never failing to either draw peals of laughter or stares of complete confusion whenever someone heard any of us say it.

"Sorry," I said, putting my phone face down on the table, "I just let some idiot on Twitter pull me into a back and forth."

"The trolls still in your mentions?" Parker asked.

I nodded with a grimace, "It was pretty much an even

mix, but I swear those folks talking shit just seem to stand out a bit more than others."

"Uh, lil ReadySetGo bout to make a comeback or nah?" Blair cracked and I groaned again.

ReadySetGo was a nickname she'd given me in undergrad after witnessing my temper go from zero to sixty in less than two seconds after an altercation with some sexist dummy who was upset about being a third string pitcher behind me. I was most often super easygoing, but when someone got up under my skin, I could not be held responsible for what came out of my mouth once the limit had been reached. I don't even remember what I'd said to that dude in the café that day, but Blair crowed about it for weeks, donning me with the nickname almost immediately. I tried keeping my temper under wraps for the most part, but every now and again RSG reared her ugly little head. I was still silently fuming about this Noah dude's claudacity. My phone chimed again with the sound the Twitter notification makes and I'd really hoped it wasn't him coming back to say yet another thing. I picked up my phone to see the mention and giggled.

@moundsandhounds: would pay really good money to see @notthegiraffe8 shut up the misogynist asshat that is @noahhhfence312

I just hit the small heart below the message and kept it moving. Putting my phone back down, I turned to the girls.

"Okay wait…where's my glass of rosé? Wooooow, I come over here to be treated like a second-class citizen, the nerve BlairBear!"

"I asked if you wanted anything when I grabbed me and P's glasses, but you were too engaged in your little back and forth with the Twitter nigga. Bottle's right there on the table and I brought you a glass in here. I'm not your servant, pour up, bih!"

I hadn't even noticed the stemless wineglass she'd set on

the table in front of where I sat on the couch. Following her directive, I filled my glass and took a long, cleansing sip.

"Ahhhh, now that's more like it. Hey sisters, what's new?" I grinned.

"Really? Don't play, heffa. Spill it!"

"Alright, fine. So y'all know how Pops was trying to get me to go to one of those damned cattle call tryouts for Team USA women's baseball team?"

"Mmmmhmmm," the girls chorused in unison.

"Well, I got a very interesting phone call from a Team USA representative who saw the viral video and told me that leadership wants me to fly down to their training facility for a chat."

"Shut the front door! Yes, G!" Blair screeched, jumping up from her chair to topple me over with a hug.

Parker's excitement was less over the top than Blair's, but equally palpable.

"How does that feel?" Parker asked, eyes shining brightly.

"It feels…I dunno, honestly…" I trailed off on a sigh.

"Are you nervous?" Blair asked.

"Fuck yes!" I exclaimed, making the two of them laugh again, "I…just…I dunno y'all. Like, this would be hella dope, playing for the national team. Making the roster, being able to represent the country internationally playing a sport at which I know I am excellent. But also…I could be setting myself up for disappointment if I assume that this invitation is more than just…hell, I don't even know what I expect the invitation to lead to, honestly. No one has said anything about me doing anything while I'm down in their offices, just that leadership was eager to meet me. For all I know, they could just be setting me up for a viral moment photo op situation that just would be self-serving and put a few more eyes on women playing a sport that is typically dominated by men."

"Or," Parker chimed in, "they could be bringing you down there to offer you a roster spot, thus making a dream that you've held from a very young age come true. C'mon, Geffri. I honestly doubt they'd fly you out just to shake some hands and take some pics. This is a very big deal, sis! What's your dad got to say about it?"

"I haven't said anything to Pops yet. I don't want his hopes to get too high. You know how he is."

"Your dad's the best, G!" Blair said, "You know we stan Mr. Robinson around here, don't even play."

Pops' feverish support for me in all aspects of my life, not just baseball, was something of legend whenever it came to Blair and Parker. Neither of them grew up with their biological dads in their lives consistently, which was something they both told me I was lucky to have. And I knew that – knew Pops was *everything* and was super grateful for him being the amazing parent he'd been all of my life, but I also did not want to be the one to deal him more disappointment. I knew he felt a way once I realized my dreams of being the first female pitcher in the MLB were nothing more than flights of fancy and I was certain he'd hoped I'd be doing more with the sport into adulthood than I had so far.

"So, when do they want you to come to…where, exactly, are you getting flewed out to?" Parker asked.

"North Carolina. Their practice facility is in some city down there…hold on I put it in my notes…" I said, picking my phone up again, noting more Twitter notifications. I cleared them from the screen without reading them and then navigated to my notes app. "Cary, North Carolina…wherever the hell that is."

"Ooh, I think that's near Raleigh," Blair piped up, "My Uncle Chip used to live down there. We never managed to make it down there and see him when he did though."

"Well I'll be down there next week to see what these people are talking about," I replied.

"That's so dope, sis. I promise I cannot wait to hear you come back and tell us how you're now the starting pitcher for Team USA's Olympic squad in 2020," Blair squealed.

"You're doing a lot, B," I said.

"Or," she countered, "am I doing just the right amount? I mean honestly, the power of positive thinking never hurt anybody, Gef!"

I held up my hands in acquiescence before she began dragging out the crystals, tarot, and the rest of her metaphysical supplies, "You're right, B. If I believe it, I can achieve it."

"Okay, you don't have to be flippant now," she grumbled in return.

"Wait a minute, let's not take it there ladies," Parker chimed in, ever the peacemaker.

"I'm not…" I started, then switched course, "so, like I said earlier…what's new with y'all?"

"Well, Park is trying daily not to mount her new employer and you know…nothing's up with me at all beyond the usual."

"Oh my God, shut up, Blair!" Parker groaned before picking up her wine glass, draining it, and refilling it.

"PDiddy boutta become a stepmama in these streets, huh?" I teased, drawing another groan from Parker as she dropped back on the couch dramatically.

"I am doing my job, nothing more, nothing less. I just need to work this job and stack my bread until I'm ready to make some serious moves."

"How is everything coming along with all of that?" I asked her, genuinely curious.

Parker, a former heptathlete, was currently on a mission to break into the Ladies Professional Golf Association. After she befell a pretty shitty end to her undergraduate career in track and field, she'd thrown herself into her golf game. Over the past couple of years, she'd been making a name for herself as a power hitter on the long drive scene. Blair, a former collegiate level soccer player, was currently coaching the same sport on the high school level in addition to teaching high school science.

"It's...coming along. Deuce is getting on my nerves per usual," she giggled, "But, my game is improving, so...that's the upside. I'm in a long drive competition down in Oklahoma in September, so we're mostly training for that now."

"When in September?" Blair chimed in, "Oklahoma's on my list, still."

"How?" I asked, incredulous.

Blair was determined to visit all fifty states and before her thirtieth birthday. Being a collegiate athlete and university level coach allowed her a fair amount of travel, so the goal was one easily attainable, but she was still picking her way through it.

"We never played the Sooners or OSU at their campuses," she shrugged, "Carolina's on my list for the same reasons...so if you want a plus one. Actually – ooh, we should do a girls trip!"

"During the week? Girl, now you know P can't get that time off on such short notice," I replied.

"When are you slated to go down to NC, Geffri?" Blair asked.

I shrugged, "I haven't received an itinerary. The guy I spoke with said that an assistant would send me an email with all of the flight and accommodation details within the next couple of days."

"Keep us posted because if we can make this work, we definitely should. It's been entirely too long since all of us have taken a trip together," Blair sighed.

"You're right, B. It's been since...what...that trip the

summer after y'all graduated and I still had one more semester to finish up?" Parker asked.

"Oh my God…that trip to Vegas…" I groaned, "Blair…are you and your future husband still Facebook friends?"

Now it was Blair's turn to groan in discontent, "Oh my God, please do not remind me of that disaster. I still can't even see the word tequila without having a violently ill reaction."

Parker and I giggled and continued teasing Blair about all of the trouble she got into when we called ourselves taking our first real trip as adults down to South Beach. We learned the hard way about moderation when it came to alcohol. I rarely touched anything harder than wine ever since. The next few hours were spent with us laying around and watching terrible movies on Netflix and finishing off the second bottle of wine we'd opened. Instead of either of us leaving to go home and sleep in our own comfortable beds, we hunkered together at Blair's, turning her living room into our sleeping area as we fell back into the rhythm of our lives when we were roommates at university. The next morning when we woke up, we were regretting the decisions of opening a third bottle of wine and snuggling together on a pallet of comforters and duvets on said living room floor.

After a quick breakfast of pancakes whipped up by Parker, I left Blair's to head over by my Pops and share with him the news about Team USA. The girls were right, I didn't need to keep him in the dark about this process until I was certain. Namely because I needed him to be there along every step of this thing, keeping my mind focused on what it needed to concentrate upon instead of spiraling out of control as I was wont to do when left to my own devices. I'd never had any shortage of confidence in my abilities, but my ultra-competitive nature left untempered overrode any positive aspects of my confidence, bringing out the worst in me. Pops always managed to talk me out of that mode though.

"Pops," I called out, using my key to let myself in.

"Speedy?" Pops called out in a strangled tone, "Er…ah… give me a minute, baby girl. I'll be right out."

I made myself comfortable, walking through the living room toward the kitchen, straight to open his fridge. I prayed that he had some water in there chilling because my mouth felt dry as hell. By the time Pops appeared, I was mainlining my second bottle of Ice Mountain, slumped at his kitchen's breakfast nook.

"Hey lil girl," he said, gruffly, "did I know you were coming over here today?"

I shook my head, still sipping the water I'd pilfered from his fridge.

"I got some news."

"You look like shit, kid. What's going on?"

"Gee, thanks Pops," I groaned, "this had nothing to do with my news. More about me still succumbing to peer pressure at my big age. Blair and Parker say hi, by the way."

"Oh, how are my girls doing?" Pops asked, his voice softening.

He'd been a father figure of sorts to them the closer that I grew to the girls. It was kinda sweet to witness and such a Pops like thing to do.

"They're good. We were doing a little celebrating."

"What were you celebrating?"

"Oh, just a little phone call I got from USA Baseball asking me to come meet with leadership," I said, nonchalantly as if we were discussing the weather.

It took a beat for the words to register in Pops' head, but the moment they did, he hopped up from where he'd been sitting, snatching me up into a tight hug.

"Hot damn, Speedy! You've done it!" he whispered tightly; his voice choked with emotion.

He pulled back briefly to look me in the eyes and I could see a light sheen of tears coating his eyes before he pulled me back into him even tighter. A sudden rush of emotion settled right at my breastplate, robbing me of my breath momentarily and I gasped for air. After a couple quick breaths in I replied.

"Thank you, daddy," I breathed, "Now…I don't even know what this meeting is about so, let's not put the cart before the horse but…"

Pops pulled back from me again, this time shaking his head and grasping my forearms in a tight grip.

"Nah, don't even complete that sentence, lil girl. We about to go down here and listen to these folks tell you how much they need your expertise, skill, and energy to join their ball club. Then you'll accept, sign a contract, and we'll go have a celebratory beer before you get to work."

"We?" I asked.

"Oh, you thought I was gonna let you go on down to… where they want you to come, Speedy?"

"Durham, North Carolina."

"Like, I was saying, you thought I was gonna let you go on down to *Durham, North Carolina* by yourself? No ma'am, I'll be booking me a flight so I can be there right alongside you as always."

"But Pops…"

"Don't 'But Pops' me, lil girl. I ain't missed a milestone in your life since the day of your birth and we ain't about to start that now. I ain't got much to do around here in retirement, so when are we taking off?"

I grinned, shrugging. "Dunno yet, I'm supposed to get an email from an assistant to the woman I spoke with that'll have the details of my itinerary and all that. Matter of fact…"

I trailed off knowing that since I didn't have my phone set to auto-push emails to my notifications that I needed to manually refresh to see if I'd gotten anything new. Right as I did that, a few emails popped up, including the one that I was looking for from the Team USA rep. I communicated the details of my trip to Pops and also sent a quick screenshot to the girls just in case they were serious about trying to turn it into a lil girls trip situation. I was going to be flown down on Thursday of this upcoming week, to meet with everyone I needed to at USA Women's Baseball bright and early on Friday morning. Pops pulled out his phone immediately to book a flight to accompany me. We sat around for a few minutes more before I left to go home and be lazy for the rest of the day as I recovered from being wine drunk.

On my way out, I noticed that the car that prevented me from parking in the driveway wasn't Pops', something curious that I'd bring up to him a little later. Right now, I barely held the energy to keep on strolling toward where my car was parked on the curb and drive home. But knowing that my luxuriously lush mattress was awaiting my aching spinal column spurred me forward. I went home, crawled into bed, pulled my comforter completely around me so that I was wrapped like a burrito, and passed the hell out.

When I awakened later that day, my phone had been buzzing incessantly for about ten minutes before I finally threw out a hand to blindly reach for where it laid on the side table next to my bed. When I finally curled my fingers around it and moved it in front of my face where I had on eye cracked to see what the hell was causing it to go haywire, I noticed that my damned Twitter had blown up again. I moaned, sitting up, to fully investigate what had happened. Apparently *SportsCenter* had gotten ahold of the video so a lot of my mentions were folks retweeting and commenting on the thread in which they'd tagged me. I muted that tweet to erase some of the notifications from clogging my phone. It was then that I'd noticed that I had a direct message from that Noah dude. Sent around the time that we had been having our back and forth yesterday, but that I hadn't seen because the girls made me put my phone down and be present in the moment that we were having. I opened the direct message and burst out laughing when I saw that it was a photograph of a tee ball set, then a question.

@noahhhfence312: are you open to a proposition?

Curious about whatever he was going to propose, I shot a reply back.

@notthegiraffe8: Depends on who's offering.

Less than twenty seconds later my phone was buzzing with Noah's reply to my DM.

@noahhhfence312: me sweetheart.

@notthegiraffe8: Hard pass. And I already told you I'm not your sweetheart.

@noahhhfence312: seriously tho. my editor has an idea that he asked me to run by you. all I'm asking is for a lil bit of your time.

@notthegiraffe8: geffri8@gmail.com. Don't waste my time.

When my phone chimed with the tone for a FaceTime call, I stared at my phone as if I'd been rendered unable to remember how to work it when the name calling displayed Noah Fence. What the hell was he FaceTiming me – without permission – for? I looked crazy as hell due to having just woken up. No way in hell I was giving him that ammunition to work with after how he'd shown his ass on the internet in my face and behind my back because I was sure he'd spewed more trash than I'd willingly taken in.

@notthegiraffe8: Why in the hell are you FaceTiming me?

@noahhhfence312: to tell you about the proposal...was... that not you replying to me earlier? you and your team should be on one accord. how do I even know this is actually you replying now?

Unthinking I navigated to my camera app and snapped a pic of myself giving him the finger with a scowl across my face and sent that.

@notthegiraffe8: Satisfied?

@notthegiraffe8: And I sent you my email address for you to send the details of your little proposal *there*. Not for you to attempt to FaceTime me.

@noahhhfence312: it's easier for me to talk it out instead of typing it. when will you be available for a call then?

@noahhhfence312: nice photo. you shoulda got that lil bit of drool on ya chin before you hit send tho.

I scrolled up and groaned. The evidence of my clearly well rested, post-nap situation was there in a small line along my chin that I hadn't even noticed before I hit send on that photo. Too annoyed with Noah and his presumption. However, my interest was still piqued about whatever he was trying to get me to agree to do, so I replied back for him to give me an hour and then call back. And then I got up, took a quick shower, tamed my hair into something that looked presentable by wrapping it in a multi-color, peacock printed scarf, and then sat there…waiting. This felt weird, waiting for a man to call me…and feeling a little ball of anxiety in my stomach about it.

Nothing about this situation was in any way romantically inclined, but the butterflies that danced in my belly felt oddly reminiscent of every time I'd finally gotten up the nerve to tell a boy in my past that I was feeling him. That heady feeling of being emboldened, yet insecure about what the reception of such a declaration would entail always stressed me the hell out. Since I was such a tomboy growing up and rarely dressed "girly", the assumption was almost always that I was into women, so the reactions to me opening up to a guy about feeling more than friendly toward him were usually filled with a lot of skepticism. Shaking off those thoughts, I flipped on my television, letting the evergreen Sunday *SVU* marathon capture my attention until my phone went off with the FaceTime tone again.

This time, at the sound of the tone, I slid my finger across to answer the call.

"Hey, Gef..." Noah said breezily, as if we were long acquainted friends.

"Noah," I returned warily.

"Well, first of all, thanks for giving me a bit of your time on this Sunday evening."

I just cocked a brow in askance as he kept right on speaking. The energy he was giving off so far in this call was so far from all of the contentiousness of the man on the internet, so I broke into his little spiel.

"Um...not that I'm complaining because I *much prefer* the more polite version of you, but...is this little change up so it'll be harder for me to say no to whatever you're proposing...or...?"

Noah chuckled and I focused in on his face for real, thinking he looked vaguely familiar but was unable to readily place him.

"The Noah Fence on Twitter is kinda of a born and bred troll. My bad, I sometimes get a bit too caught up in the heel character I play online when I'm egged on by the audience."

"That's...a little sad," I said without thinking.

Noah inhaled sharply, "Ouch, careful, miss lady...I'm supposed to be the one with the barbs."

Hearing those two words made it click. "You were at the game. *That game*," I emphasized.

"Uh yeah, I said that on Twitter."

I shook my head quickly, "Nah nah, I mean we met...

kinda. When that man almost took me completely out the game on my way to get beers. You...gave me my hat back."

"Oh shit, that was you?" Noah said.

I nodded.

"You look different without all of the..." Noah trailed off, gesturing his hands around his close-cropped hair, I assume to mimic the fullness of my hair whenever I let it just breathe its natural state.

"You look different when your companion isn't trying to damn near kill me," I shot back.

Noah chuckled lowly, pulling his lower lip between his teeth. "My bad, my brother and I tend to act like overgrown kids whenever we see each other. He and my sister in law are in town visiting and we hadn't seen each other in person in almost two years since bro had been on a tour."

"I remember her checking the hell out of y'all for bumping into me," I giggled.

"Yeah, she was pretty pissed that you pulled that disappearing act because she really wanted to make that up to you. Nate and I had to hear about it for the rest of the game. That was a *long* afternoon."

"Got to be more careful," I quipped with a shrug, "Anyway, you're off topic and my time is money. So...what's your little proposition or whateva?"

"Well, one of my editors over at Atop the Mound saw our back and forth and the challenge that I issued and you, in your right mind, declined due to fear of embarrassment—"

"Hold fast, playa. Nobody but you would be embarrassed if we went head to head, trust and believe."

"Oh, I *like* her," a voice purred in the background.

"Of course, you would Chelsea, y'all are the same kind of cocky..." Noah shot back, "Didn't I tell you that I was on a serious phone call and not to disturb me though?"

"Rude...I just wanted to know where your plunger was.

Nate's had a bit of an…accident."

"Goddamnit!" Noah growled, "Geffri, I'm so sorry, can you give me a couple minutes?"

"Sure," I said, already tuned back into *SVU*.

Less than ninety seconds had passed before Noah was back in front of his computer, huffing a breath. "Sorry about that. Anyway…let me speed this along, I've taken up too much of your time. My editor would like us to film a video pitting us head to head in a variety of competitive situations – none baseball – and seeing who would really come out the victor."

"Hm," I mused, "Sounds interesting. Would I be able to choose any of these activities?"

Noah shook his head, "All of them would be chosen by the *AtM* editorial staff."

"And how do I know they won't pick things that are more suited toward you being the winner in the end?"

"You just have to trust me, sw—er…Geffri," Noah replied charmingly.

"Ehhhhh, I dunno about that. But hey, I'm curious enough to give you a soft yes. I would, however, love for you all to send over a proper proposal of what all this video would entail, when you're trying to shoot it, and all of that."

Noah nodded. "Okay okay, bet. I'll reach out to Griffin, the EIC, and get back to you once he gives me some more detail?"

"Sounds like a plan."

"Aight, I'ma let you go, then. I'll be in touch."

"Alright Noah, you have a good night."

"You too, Geffri."

"Oh," I called out just before we disconnected, "get ready to be embarrassed in front of millions. I don't lose…ever."

"May the odds ever be in your favor, Miss Robinson," Noah teased with a grin before disconnecting the call.

THIRD INNING

"*D*addy, please!" I groaned as he changed his outfit for the fourth time this morning.

He had to know I was exasperated since I rarely called him Daddy, usually in moments charged with emotion or I needed to snap him back to reality. This time it was the latter. Hell, you'd think that he was the one who had someone to impress today instead of me. We had made it down to North Carolina late last night after a few flight delays and I was dragging this morning, having awakened after only having about four hours of sleep. I mistakenly thought that I saw a Starbucks in the hotel lobby but was fooled. It was a coffee shop that "proudly served Starbucks". Needing the caffeine anyway, I ordered a small cup of coffee that I barely had two sips of before tossing it in the trash. The person responsible for the brewing of those beans clearly hated humanity. The coffee was burnt terribly, settling upon my tongue with an angrily acrid flavor profile. That lack of caffeine plus Pops being his usual persnickety self this morning had me on edge. I glanced over at the clock, noting that we had about an hour before I needed to meet with the Team USA reps and tried once again to hurry Pops along. It only took an additional ten minutes of harassing before we piled into our rental and I hit the road in search of a decent cup of coffee before we'd settle at the Team USA offices.

Soon though, we were walking through the doors of an unassuming office building in the middle of office park land in Durham. While the training facility for USA Baseball was in Cary – about half an hour away – where all of the business was handled happened right here in Durham. I was meeting with the women's program director, team manager and the pitching coach. The pitching coach, Ray, was the one who'd actually seen my video on Twitter and brought it to the rest of the team to check out. He was thoroughly impressed with my ability and thought that I would be a valuable asset to the team overall.

"Geffri," Ray greeted me warmly as he walked into the reception area.

He ushered my dad and I into his office, letting us know that we'd be joined shortly by the team manager/coach Molly and the program director, Gretchen. It boded well for me to see a program that was an offshoot of a male dominated industry have women in prominent leadership roles, not as figureheads. Ray began our conversation by explaining the program and then concluded with how he thought I could bring a bit of a different flavor to the squad. It was at this time that Molly and Gretchen peeked in to join us. After quick introductions, Ray began his spiel again.

"I have to tell you, Geffri, if I'm being perfectly honest – I was completely amazed by what looks like ambidexterity? I'm not tripping right? You definitely pitched with both hands in that contest video, right?"

I couldn't help the grin that lit my face, unbidden. In all of the talk about that video since it'd gone viral, Ray was the first person to comment on what had been my secret weapon from my sophomore year of high school onward. I'd grown up being a lefty pitcher since that's my dominant hand for doing everything in life, but I told my dad that I felt that it limited my chances for really taking my game to the next level and so he'd found me a private coach to work with to help me develop my form for pitching with my right hand as well. It was something that not many folks had the capability to do…and do well, at that, but it was definitely something that made me stand out from the field.

I nodded, "Yeah, it's a lil something Pops and I added to my arsenal in high school in order to raise my profile."

"I'm honestly shocked a bigger deal wasn't made of it. But I think it's because you transitioned so smoothly that somebody really had to be inspecting the hell out of that video to pick up on it. So, I guess here is where I admit that I ran it back enough that I think I definitely contributed a hefty sum to the million plus views that the clip had racked up on social media," Ray laughed.

"We love the idea of having a secret weapon in the midst," Gretchen chimed in, "So…let us just say it flat out instead of talking all around it. We'd like to extend to you a spot on the roster, Geffri."

Hearing those words from her mouth immediately made my eyes well with tears that I tried but failed at holding back. I tried discreetly wiping my eyes, as my dad spoke up to inform me that he'd told me so and to tell Gretchen that of course I would be accepting. I shook my head at his forwardness, knowing that it was nothing but eagerness at him seeing me reach another height that he hadn't scaled in his sports career. I couldn't even be mad because I knew how immensely proud, he was and couldn't help himself. I sniffled a little before finally chiming in.

"Well, I honestly cannot say that I was certain that you all would be offering me a roster spot upon this visit at all, but Pops got two things right. Only one of them is important to you all though…but before I can completely accept, can we go over the particulars of the expectations and schedule? I just want to make sure I have no schedule conflicts."

"Absolutely," Molly chimed in, "And even if you do have any conflicts, don't let that bar you from saying yes. You…are gonna say yes, right?"

"She absolutely will," Pops piped up again.

Everyone in the room cracked up at his intrusion.

"I absolutely will," I parroted after we'd calmed from our laughter.

"Excellent," Ray said, extending a hand my way, "welcome to the team. I look forward to working with you over this summer."

From there, Molly and Gretchen took over the lead of the conversation, explaining to me the details I'd asked for more clarity on regarding my commitment and their expectations. After getting the initial contract details sorted out, the three of them took Pops and I took take a look at the training complex for all of Team USA's different national baseball teams. It was a stunning campus, replete with one stadium field and three practice fields that were all maintained to meet Major League Baseball standards. I was most impressed by the stadium field's set up because in addition to the field being beautifully maintained, it also included a nice sized spectator area, which included two suites, a complete sound room, scorer's room, and press box. I wandered away from the crowd of those four, heading straight toward the mound in the center of the field.

"You wanna throw a few?" Ray called out once they realized I'd stepped away from where they stood conversing.

I shook my head, "Just checking out the view."

Ray shook his head right back at me. "Nah, I recognize that glint in your eye. Gimme a couple min."

With that he dashed away into the dugout, returning with a glove, two balls, and a catcher's mitt. He dropped the catcher's mitt near home plate then made his way over to me.

"Let's see what you got," Ray said, jogging over to hand me the glove and balls.

"If you insist," I laughed, briefly cracking my knuckles before I grabbed the items from Ray.

I waited until he was positioned back behind the plate before winding up. The first ball I kinda whiffed a bit, resulting in a pitch that was way outside, but still had some heat on it if the slight grimace on Ray's face when he snagged it was any indication. What was only supposed to be a quick couple pitches, ended up being fifteen minutes of Ray and I going back and forth, with him offering little bits of correction to my form that he noticed. The manner in which he communicated and the way I responded to his criticisms let me know that this environment was going to be miles better than some of the team environments I'd been in prior.

After we got back to the office where Pops and I were parked, he and I grabbed a bite to eat before heading back to the hotel. We had mid-afternoon flight back home, so I'd requested late check-out for our room so we couldn't have to futz with our luggage and all of that on the way to the meeting this morning. I was glad that I had the foresight to do that because it allowed me to also be able to catch a quick nap before we had to be up and out. Pops hadn't stopped grinning since we left Team USA's offices. Unlike usual, he hadn't said much, but over the course of the day I'd see him just staring at me and grinning. That proud glint in his eyes never failed to make me feel like I was incapable of failure. On the flight home, I used the inflight Wi-Fi to log onto the internet and saw that two pieces of information that I'd been anticipating had already hit my inbox. The first, and more pressing, was all of the info I needed for Team USA, including my flight details to come to Texas where the team would be practicing until we took off for the international tournament that we'd be competing in and the schedule for the team's tournament and exhibition rotation. The majority of the games would be happening in early to late-August, which was great for my schedule since we didn't get back into school until after Labor Day. It meant that I could revel in spending my summer pouring into Team USA and giving my all without the stresses of teacher duty weighing on my shoulders. I also, however, still wanted to keep my administration in the loop, so I shot off a quick email to them explaining the opportunity I'd been given and attached a screenshot of the schedule with dates, so they could get back to me with any potential they saw for conflict since our report back date still hadn't been cemented for some strange reason.

They wanted me to come down to Texas the first week in August, which was just over a week away. They'd just extended invitations to a total of almost forty women to come to the National Team Development Program. A lot of these girls and women had competed for Team USA in some capacity and would be whittled down into the twenty woman roster that would represent the country in international competition. When I spoke with Ray, Molly, and Gretchen, they assured me that I had a roster spot, but that I needed to be there during all stages of this process to get to know the women I'd be playing with eventually. I was looking forward to the experience honestly. I'd never really experienced what it was like to be on a team with all women until I started coaching and even then—my feelings were wholly different as coach versus an actual player. I was looking forward to bonding with the women on the team as well as hopefully bringing home a gold at the international tournament.

There was also an email, as promised, from Noah about this little silly challenge thing that he and his editors wanted to set up. The subject line of *You Are Cordially Invited...to get your ass kicked* let me know exactly what I was getting myself into here. I chuckled slightly before opening it up to read the details. Since we both lived in the same area and he wouldn't have to travel, his editor wanted to get our little segment filmed within the next week or so in order to go live in *Atop the Mound* the week after that. I had no scheduling conflicts, so that was an easy yes to give. Especially since I was eager to hand Noah his ass in whatever they chose for us to compete against one another doing. I honestly had been looking forward to striking his ass out repeatedly, but since they insisted that anything baseball related wouldn't be included. Scrolling through the email some of the suggestions they chose were a game of horse, bowling, golfing, and shooting pool. I was amenable to anything and let them know as much in my return email informing Noah that I would be taking his challenge.

By the time I'd replied to Noah, my principal had also emailed me back, gushing over my opportunity to play with Team USA and noting that there wouldn't be any scheduling conflicts since she'd excuse me for our official report back date, allowing me to come in and prep during the last week in August instead of taking the entire last two weeks of the month as every other teacher would. I briefly wondered how she'd explain this decision before remembering that every night she laid down next to the district's superintendent who'd back her no matter what. I still didn't know how they navigated that conflict of interest but was thankful that it worked to my advantage at this juncture.

Finishing up responding to my emails, I navigated over to

Twitter to scroll my timeline for the hour I had left in this flight. Pops had knocked out as soon as we boarded – typical behavior – so I had to find my own entertainment. Luckily some of the hullabaloo from my little viral video had died down so my mentions on Twitter weren't looking as crazy as usual. I did notice, however, that Noah had hit the follow button recently. Out of politeness, I clicked his profile and followed him back, which led to me just aimlessly scrolling down his timeline. He wasn't lying when he said he was a bit of a troll online, he had smoke for everybody. All of his takes weren't terrible, I thought while reading his assessment of a recent scandal about stealing signs that had been all the rage in #baseballtwitter. I went from scrolling his timeline to clicking over to *Atop the Mound* to read anything he'd written, which led me to his personal site – *brothas&bats*, which was a site dedicated to highlighting historical and current Black men in the MLB. His most recent piece was about the importance of CC Sabathia to the game of baseball and the impact his retirement would have on the game going forward. It was a very thoughtful piece, exemplifying an acute intelligence and clear passionate obsession with the game of baseball. It made me curious about his entire story which led to me reading about a pretty gruesome car accident that he was in during undergrad that left him with two broken legs and no chance of returning as the star of his university baseball team, let alone progressing to play in the majors. Given how close we were in age and from the same general area, I thought it was strange that I'd never heard of Noah until he appeared in my notifications last week.

Soon the plane was landing, and I was dropping Pops back off at his place. I noticed he was doing a lot of texting on the twenty-minute drive across town and when we arrived the unfamiliar car from the other day was in the driveway again.

"Pops, whose car is that?" I asked, hoping it sounded casual.

"You…uh…got a minute to come in?" he replied.

My brow wrinkled in confusion to his obfuscating. "Yeah."

I cut the car off and trailed him into the house once he'd grabbed his duffel from my back seat. We had just crossed the threshold of the front door when a throaty voice crooned, "Welcome back, baby…"

I looked past Pops to see some woman clad in a whole lot of nothing draped against the banister of the stairs that led to the upstairs. Almost instantly she realized my father wasn't alone, shrieked and ran up the stairs. Pops sighed deeply, ran a hand over his bald head, and turned to me.

"Well, that certainly wasn't how I wanted y'all to meet. Gimme a minute, Speedy," he said, without waiting for an answer from me as he ambled up the stairs after who I assume was his lady.

Perplexed, I sat down in the living room until I heard the telltale creaking of the stairs that led me know that someone was descending. Seconds later Pops appeared with a fully dressed version of the woman from earlier at his side.

"Spee…Geffri, this is Brenda. Bren, this is my baby girl," Pops said as they walked into the living room.

The woman, Brenda, rushed forward sweeping me up into a scented hug, "Oh it's so good to finally meet you, Geffri. I've heard so much about you."

"I…can't really say the same," I replied honestly, "But it's nice to meet you as well Miss Brenda."

"That's all me," Pops broke in, "I wasn't sure how you'd take me dating again, baby girl since it had been us for so long."

"Pops, please," I huffed, "I've been lowkey praying that

you'd find somebody so you can stay outta my business so much."

"Hey!" he laughed.

"Kidding of course, old man. We'll have to have lunch or dinner one of these days, so I can get to know Miss Brenda a little better."

Brenda's eyes sparkled at that statement. "Absolutely, sweetheart! I've told Leon we needed to set something up for a few months now."

At that, my eyes widened a bit. If she'd been telling him that he needed to introduce us for months, Pops had been holding out for a minute. The sheepish look that covered his features let me know that he knew I'd figured him out, but I wanted him to know I wasn't upset. I thought it was overdue, honestly. He'd given so much to me over the years that he deserved to live his life for himself now, finding happiness wherever he saw fit. And if the twinkle in his eyes as he sidled closer to Brenda and wrapped her in an embrace was any indication, she was definitely a key to his happiness.

"Aight, fine. We'll sit down later this week. Does Thursday afternoon work for you, Speedy?" Pops offered.

"Works for me," I agreed with a grin, "My flight down to Texas isn't until later that evening."

"Me too," Brenda chimed up.

"Perfect! Pops, I wanna put in a request for your white chicken lasagna."

"Who said I was cooking?"

"It's only right, old man," I cracked, "I'll bring dessert. See y'all then."

I left them to whatever they were about to get into; anxious to get home and do absolutely nothing. During the summers I usually taught, but this year I decided to take a true summer break and spend my time doing whatever I saw fit. A lot of my time was spent binge watching all of the television shows I'd heard my friends talking about so often, but I'd not wanted to begin watching in the middle so I waited until they had concluded and then watched the entire thing all at once. Currently I was bingeing "The Office" for the second time. I sat laughing at Michael Scott's ineptitude and scrolling social media again when I saw a tweet from Noah.

@noahhhfence312: welp, ladies and gents, it turns out that @notthegiraffe8 really does want that smoke. stay tuned...

This negro, I thought before I retweeted his tweet, adding my own commentary.

@notthegiraffe8: Stay tuned to see little @noahhhfence312 humbled by a girl. #uh82cit

His little tweet sent me straight to my email to see if they'd sent me concrete details about this sideshow that I'd agreed to take part in. They had, in fact. The email outlined the entirety of their agenda for the contest. The shoot was to take place on Wednesday of this week, with us meeting up just after midday at a local park for the first of three activities in the challenge. The first activity was going to be a one on one game of street basketball out at the park. We'd be playing ones and twos, with the first to make it to thirteen by a margin of two points or more being crowned the winner. The last two activities would take place indoors at a local watering hole named *Smitty's* – darts and a game of pool. I had to chuckle to myself because despite having no actual control over the composition of this contest, I felt very confident that I'd be walking away a victor as all of these activities were things in which I was well-versed and had mopped the floor with my fair share of asses at all of them. This thing with Noah would be light work.

FOURTH INNING

"So...you want me and the kids to be there as like... your emotional support cheer squad?" Parker asked skeptically.

It was the morning of my showdown with Noah and I woke up feeling uncharacteristically...nervous. I couldn't quite pinpoint why, but knowing he was coming into the game with at least one additional person there with vested interest for him to win, I felt like I needed to even the odds. I would have asked Blair, but she was out of town on the annual Conway Family Vacation and wouldn't be back for another three days. Pops would have been too overbearing since his competitive streak ran just as deep as my own and I didn't have any other folks I'd really want to be there and in my corner beyond Pops, Blair, and Parker. I knew it was a stretch since she had two little ones under the age of five for whom she was entrusted with the daily care, but I tried throwing a bone anyway.

"I mean...don't you normally take the kids out to do activities anyway? And we'll be at a park so like..." I trailed off.

I could hear Parker heave a sigh and I knew I got her. I silently celebrated before she even confirmed that she would be there.

"What time is it at again? You know we have to pick up Chloe from school by 2:15," Parker said.

"Oh, we should be done way before then! I'm supposed to meet Noah and his people in the park by quarter of one. Since it's just a simple pick-up game of basketball, it shouldn't take more than half an hour or so…"

"Fine. Me, Dyl, and Dede will be there," Parker grumbled.

"Thank you thank you thank you! See, that's why you're my favorite over Blair!"

"Yeah yeah, if B was in town, she'd be your favorite right now," Parker snickered.

I said nothing to refute the assertion because it wasn't off base. Whichever one of them was the one to do my bidding usually earned the title of favorite. In all honesty, they were permanently tied for the title of favorite friend in my life due to our bonds in undergrad. We were just a couple hours out from when I needed to meet up at the park, but I wanted to get some shots up before meeting up with Noah. I hadn't played ball competitively in a while and just wanted to make sure my jumper was as wet as it once was. Pops had a hoop connected to his garage, so I showered and made my way over there to get some practice in. I didn't bother going inside, just put in the code to raise the garage and dug around until I found a ball. I'd been shooting around from various places in the driveway for about half an hour when I heard Pops pull up. As he approached where I stood, I faked a pass in his direction before driving to the hoop and laying the ball up.

"Speedy, still got those hops huh?" Pops smiled.

"A lil bit…" I giggled, dribbling my way toward him to

give him a quick embrace, "You got a game of horse in you or nah?"

Pops shook his head, begging off. "I'm tired, Speedy."

"Long night at Ms. Brenda's huh?" I joked, doubling over in laughter when Pops eyes widened to comical proportions.

"Stay in your lane, lil girl," he said once he got himself together.

"I'm joking, Pops. And I meant what I said the other day, too. I'm happy for you, old man."

"Yeah yeah," he replied gruffly heading into the house, "Aye, make sure you wipe the floor with that young man who was talkin' all that smack today."

"Wait…how did you…?"

"Twitter is free and for the public, lil girl," Pops replied with a wink.

A few more minutes of shooting around and the nerves I'd felt earlier had dissipated, leaving me feeling good as I got in my car and made my way over to the park where we'd be shooting. By the time I pulled up Parker and the kids were already there on the playground. I strolled over to where she was pushing Dede on the swings, stopping along the way to give Dylan a quick high five as he ran past me through the faux pirate ship that the playground had been fashioned into.

"PDiddy!" I greeted her with a quick hug and moved in to tickle little Dede in greeting as well.

"Hey girl…how you feel?" Parker asked now, "You look cute."

"Oh, this old thing?" I asked, gesturing toward the brand-new Nike gear I'd purchased for the express means of looking cute on film as I wiped the floor with Noah. "Thanks boo! I'm…less nervous than earlier if that's what you're getting at. Thank you, again, for coming out here with me."

"Oh girl you know it's nothing," she replied back with a dismissive wave of her hand, "Plus I finally went back to see the sh...stuff buddy was talking on Twitter and I knew I had to grab a front row seat to you completely destroying him in real time."

"He was talking mad trash, right?" I agreed.

"Too much. Better hope he can back it up," Parker laughed.

We moved on in the conversation talking about everything that was unfolding with her quest to snag a spot on a golf tour and her...growing attraction to the dad of the kids she nannied for. Apparently, the feeling was mutual if I was interpreting the coded language that she used to describe the feeling around the house correctly. I took a moment to just observe her demeanor and for the first time in a while, Parker looked *happy*. She'd been through the wringer over the past few years, so I was glad to see her coming out of it. From our vantage point, I could see when Noah and his folks arrived and started setting up for the shoot. I saw them shooing some folks off one of the basketball courts and setting up their equipment. I nudged Parker, who in turn gathered a pouting Dylan and sleepy Dede and followed me over to the courts.

"But Miss Parker I wasn't done playin'," Dylan whined as we made our way over to the courts.

"And we had a deal, Mr. Pickles. Remember I told you that Miss Geffri needed our support today? And then what?"

"And that we would get ice cream after," Dylan replied.

"So, you wanna go back to playing? Because if so, we can do that. But then we won't have done our job and showed up to support a friend, so no ice cream as reward."

Dylan's little face scrunched up as he weighed his options.

"I want ice cream," he finally replied.

"Then let's go," Parker said, a note of finality in her voice that snapped Dylan into formation.

"Ok stepmom!" I whispered earning a glare from Parker.

"You make me sick. I'll take these kids and go back to the playground," Parker gritted out under her breath as we got closer to Noah and his folks.

"You wouldn't," I gasped.

"Try me," she grinned before settling herself and the kids on the bench alongside the basketball courts.

Noah turned in our direction and his handsome face contorted into a cocky smirk as he approached where I stood next to Parker and the kids. As he strolled over, I heard Parker whispering that I hadn't said anything about how fine my opponent was. I couldn't even reply to her assessment because he was right up in our space in little to no time.

"This is...quite the entourage you got, Geffri," Noah quipped, "If I knew you were bringing a such a savage crew, I woulda had my editor spring for craft service. Hooked y'all right on up with all the *Capri Suns* and *Goldfish* you could stand."

I rolled my eyes. "Noah," I said in lieu of a greeting.

"Aw, don't be like that, sweetheart. Introduce me to your posse."

I rolled my eyes at him before turning to Parker and the kids, "This is one of my best friends, Parker and the kids she nannies for – Dylan and Ardelia. Guys, this is Noah."

Parker smiled in acknowledgement and Dylan, still pouting from being taken from his fun time playing on the playground, completely ignored us. The baby had fallen asleep in Parker's arms and for a moment I felt bad for asking her to bring them out here. I'd completely ignored their comfort for the sake of having some of my own. I was just about to open my mouth to tell Parker that she and the kids could bounce when Noah nudged me along.

"Come on," Noah said, wrapping an arm around my shoulders, "I'll introduce you to my crew and then we can get going."

We walked over to the beneath the basketball hoop where three folks stood chatting.

"Aye y'all, this is Geffri," Noah said breaking into their convo with no preamble, pointing at each person he went on, "This is Sarai, Jonah, and Will."

We shook hands and they ran down how this would all go down. Jonah and Sarai would both be recording while Noah and I played while Will was there to supervise them. Noah would also be attempting to interview me while we were playing, which should be interesting.

"If you're ready to go, we can get this popping off," Noah said, snagging the basketball from the ground where it lay at our feet and twirling it on a finger.

I snatched the ball mid-twirl, dribbled down court and said, "Let the games begin!"

I'd thrown on a lightweight hoodie over the tank and leggings I wore, but knew I needed to shed it before we began playing and I started to work up a sweat. Jogging over to where Parker and the kids sat, I snatched it off to leave it on the bench. Dylan looked to be on the cusp of one of his infamous meltdowns that Parker had previously told me about, so I gave her an out if she wanted to pack up the kids and get out of here. She shook her head fervently though, insisting that she needed to see how this all played out. Before I could ask what she meant by that, I heard Noah calling out for me. When I turned back to tell him to give me a minute, my mouth damn near dropped to the ground. For some reason, he'd taken off the t-shirt he'd been wearing and stood with his hands braced on his hips only wearing a pair of ball shorts that rode low on his waist. The lack of shirt showed off the bronze-colored, muscled deliciousness of Noah's body.

"Shit, goddamn, motherfucker," I whispered before I could contain myself, causing Parker to laugh out loud.

"Pick it up, Gef," Parker teased.

"Pick what up?"

"Your lower lip, sis."

"Shut up," I said, turning to jog over to the middle of the court.

"You ready, Jonah?" Noah asked the guy with the camera standing in front of us as I reached them.

"Where's...your shirt?" I asked, frowning to cover up the feelings of intense lust that now filtered through me as I stood within arm's reach.

He looked even better up close. *Have mercy.*

"We're playing streetball, right? That's always shirts versus skins...unless you wanna be skins?" Noah offered a look of perfect innocence on his face that betrayed the lecherous tone of his suggestion. He kept his eyes stayed on me; his lower lip tucked between his teeth as he looked for a response. I blushed under the intensity of his gaze before sucking in a breath and rolling my eyes.

"L-let's just get this over with," I tried to reply breezily, but my slight stammer at the beginning betrayed the cool I fought to maintain with my facial expression.

"Aight Jonah count us down," Noah said, grinning in my direction.

A brief countdown from ten and our shoot commenced. Noah began the interview portion of this giving some background on our little Twitter back and forth, as well as some of my athletic history. I was impressed since he'd clearly done his homework on me as he ran down my high school and undergraduate accolades. Of course, it wasn't completely sweet because as soon as he ran down all of my accolades, he ended by saying how all of those things wouldn't mean much when he proved his superiority on the court this afternoon.

"You talk a lotta shit for someone who spends most of his day being a troll on the internet," I said, dribbling the ball I'd had clutched under my arm and then passed it in his direction, "Check up."

Noah dribbled the ball a little, trying to be fancy and lost his dribble briefly before recovering and passing the ball back in my direction.

"Ladies first, sweetheart."

From there the game was on. I dribbled the ball out to half court as Noah kept talking directly to the camera, breaking down the preset rules of our game before making his way closer to me to begin playing. Since he'd insisted that I have possession of the ball first, I took advantage of it, pulling up from damn near half court after he'd checked the ball and letting one fly. As the ball swished through the net I asked with a smirk, "We playin' keeps right?"

"Oh…okay, somebody came with a lil game, bet," Noah said, throwing the ball back to where I awaited it at the top of the key.

From there it was on and we engaged in a super charged back and forth – trading baskets from all over the court. I'd forgotten that the cameras were even there as I talked shit to Noah while backing him down to the basket and floating a jumper over his outstretched hands attempting to defend.

"You can't guard me," I crowed, backpedaling and dancing at the same time.

Parker and the kids were on the sideline cheering their faces off. With my last bucket, I'd gone up on Noah eleven to nine. Only needing two more points to seal the win, I dribbled the ball at half court weighing the options. I could pull up from the arc and shoot, effectively ending the game with one shot or I could keep driving on him straight to the hoop. I could tell that despite all of the trash talk that steadily spewed from his mouth, Noah was a bit winded and my jumper had been iffy all day.

FOURTH INNING • 51

"You need a water break or somethin', Robinson? C'mon," Noah called out, still down court near the rim.

"I'm waiting on you to play some of that infamous lock down d you claim to have," I shot back, still dribbling the ball as I surveyed the court.

"If you wanted the d, all you had to do was ask, sweetheart," Noah said, closing in on me.

I stumbled, momentarily stunned by the double entendre before catching my footing again and making the decision to shut his ass up with a dagger. I dribbled once, twice, as he advanced before I stepped back behind the three-point line and shot the ball.

"And that's game!" I called as the ball sailed through the hoop, making zero contact with the rim, just swishing through the net.

Parker and the kids were on their feet, screaming like I'd just made the winning shot for a national championship and I ran over to them on the sidelines. I hoisted Dylan up in my arms in celebration as Parker led him and his baby sister in chanting "MVP" over and over. Slowly, Noah made his way over to the sideline where we stood being obnoxious with his camera crew in tow. As soon as he was in range Dylan yelled, "You got beat by a girl!" causing all of us to fall apart in laughter.

"Please tell me you got that," Noah said to Jonah who nodded.

"Good game," Noah said, "Though I believe your foot was on the line on that last shot, so technically…"

I rolled my eyes, stepping right into his face, close enough that we were damn near chest to chest, "Whatever, man. I won fair and square. Don't be mad."

A look I couldn't quite decipher quickly crossed Noah's face before he schooled his features into a more neutral visage. He chuckled, a low and rumbly sound that set off a round of butterflies low in my belly, before biting down on his lower lip and assessing me from head to toe. A tingly sort of feeling spread throughout my body, following the path that his eyes slowly took down my form.

"I'll let you have it, but don't get too comfortable. I'ma wax that ass before the night is through. See you at *Smitty's* at five?"

"*Smitty's* at five it is," I replied a little breathlessly, nodding before turned back to Parker and the kids, effectively dismissing Noah.

When I looked over at her, Parker's face was covered in a mischievous look.

"What, PD?"

"Geffri, you in danger, girl."

"Oh please, I can beat him again with one hand tied behind my back," I scoffed.

Parker slowly shook her head, "Nah, that ain't why you in danger."

"Care to elucidate?" I sniped causing Parker to laugh in my face.

"Oh girl, you're breaking out the SAT words, which lets me know you already know why you in danger. Be safe outchea," she said with a pat to my shoulder, "We've gotta get outta here to pick up Chlo, but um...*please* let me know how the rest of this day turns out, expeditiously. I need to live vicariously."

I scrunched my face in confusion, "Vicariously through a game of darts and pool?"

Parker shook her head, "Nah, vicariously after that man waxes your a-s-s like he promised before he left."

"He was talking about in the games," I protested weakly.

"Mmmmhmm," Parker replied knowingly, "Like I said... I'll be awaiting a report. Kids, say bye to Miss Geffri."

Both of the kids dutifully waved as they headed back up

toward the playground where our cars were parked. Meanwhile I mulled over Parker's parting words. *Noah hadn't been thinking about me in any other way beyond a competitor, right?* I thought trying to recall our interactions so far. He'd said a few things that could be interpreted as flirtatious, but nothing that overtly spoke to him being attracted toward me or anything. I was the queen in misinterpreted signals, most often mistaking friendly overtures to mean much more which usually led to my disappointment. Parker was imagining things because I hadn't picked up on any of the vibes that she claimed Noah was sending out. Hell, I wished I had because he was *all caps fine*, something I'd noticed even before all of this began when he'd returned my cap at the ballpark. Despite that observation, I knew that it'd be foolish of me to allow myself think anything beyond him being attractive because my track record showed that the men I wanted most often did not want me.

FIFTH INNING

When I walked into *Smitty's* it was uncharacteristically quiet. I was used to hearing the jukebox blaring tunes or audio from one of the four TVs in the joint blaring. Instead, I just heard the hum of conversation between the patrons who were seated around the bar. It didn't take me long to find Noah, Jonah, and Sarai. I walked over to where they were situated in the back of the bar where I was greeted warmly by a grinning Sarai.

"Hey, Geffri! You ready to embarrass Big Mouth some more?"

I giggled, "Hey Sarai…you already know it."

"Damn, Rai, I thought you were on my side," Noah grumbled, ambling over and standing between Sarai and me.

She shoved him out of the way before retorting, "Tuh! Sisters over misters, clown."

He shot her a look of irritation and I laughed at them continuing to go back and forth like siblings. You could tell that they honestly had a good rapport, but Sarai was loving the fact that I'd managed to humble him earlier in the day.

"Aye Noah let's see if this works," Jonah called out, redirecting Noah's attention. He shot me a head nod in acknowledgement before he and Noah futzed around with the small lighting rig that they'd set up between the dart boards and pool tables.

"I told them as soon as we walked in that it would be too dark to film in here, but they swear they got it," Sarai grumbled.

"You know how men can be though," I laughed, and she nodded in fierce agreement.

"I'm just glad that Will's ass is gone. He's so freaking overbearing. I honestly don't even know why he was there this morning. I can keep these two knuckleheads on task without additional oversight," Sarai continued, seemingly talking to herself more than me so I just let her rant on. After a few minutes more, she shook her head, laughing at herself. "My bad, girl. I'm just ranting on and on…you'll have to excuse me. I guess I needed to vent."

I shook my head, "Oh girl, if *no one else* knows the trouble of working in a highly testosterone male dominated work environment, *I do*. You do not have to apologize or asked to be excused at all. I feel you. Let it out."

Sarai grinned and thanked me for being so understanding as Noah and Jonah walked over to where we stood.

"Ok, Rai. I think we got it. Come see if this works for you from all angles," Jonah said.

When they walked away, Noah started back up with his shit talking.

"It's not too late for you to throw in the towel, Robinson."

"Cute, but I'd rather beat you at all of your own games captured on film in perpetuity," I grinned.

Noah stepped even closer to me, hooking a finger in one of my belt loops and leaning down to say, "I didn't pick *Smitty's* randomly, sweetheart. I'm intimately familiar with this bar and these games. No way in hell I'm losing with home-court advantage."

I sucked in a shuddering breath at our proximity, trying not to succumb to the weakening in my knees, stepping back before I responded, "You've neglected to take into account one thing, Mr. Fence."

"Oh yeah, what's that?" Noah asked, that damned bottom lip of his pulled between his teeth as he lazily glanced down upon me.

"What are two of a pitcher's greatest strengths? Hand eye coordination out of this world and a steady hand. Both of which are in my possession. Therefore, placing *me* at the advantage here."

"Y'all ready?" Jonah asked, his voice closer than I expected which made me jump a little.

"Born," Noah responded before strolling off toward the dart board leaving me to stare after him.

"Aight, so what are we playing?" I asked when I'd made my way to where Noah and Sarai stood, "Three oh one? Five oh one? Seven oh one?"

Noah smirked, likely caught off guard that I knew official darts game names, then shook his head, "Nah, but shout out to you for doing your research, though. We're gonna play a game you're super familiar with…or at least should be…baseball."

I scrunched my face in confusion, "Uh…you do realize we're indoors and there's no ball and bat."

Noah chuckled before explaining to me the rule of dart baseball. We'd face each other in nine "innings", each having three darts or "strikes" to attempt to "score" during the inning. We were to aim for the number of whatever "inning" it was in order to score. So, for example, if we were in the third "inning" of this game and one of my darts hit a six instead of a three, that wouldn't count toward my score at all.

FIFTH INNING • 57

The person with the highest score at the end of the game would win. It sounded simple enough, so when Noah asked if I had any questions, I shook my head, reaching for the darts that he extended in my direction. Sarai would be keeping score since we'd be mostly stationary there was no need for multicamera angles, Jonah would just move around as he saw fit to capture us while we were playing.

"Ladies first again?" I asked, grinning in Noah's direction as he shook his head.

"Nah, fuck that. Loser leads," he replied back, and we all burst into laughter, "Let's go, Vanna Black. Get that scoreboard up."

Sarai rolled her eyes, but did as he said, moving toward the chalk board that was used for keeping score and writing our names along the top with the numbers one through nine alone the long edge of the chalkboard.

"Alright loser, you're up," Sarai announced after she'd created our "scoreboard".

"Ha ha," Noah said humorlessly, lining up behind the skinny piece of black tape on the floor that designated the distance from which we were to launch our darts.

He threw his darts in quick succession, two of them landing in the number one segment. He cockily swaggered aside as I moved forward for my first turn. Despite my intense concentration, none of my darts landed where they'd needed to in this first inning and the subsequent inning after that.

"Mighty quiet now, Robinson," Noah crowed, "Aye, Rai. What that score looking like?"

"Eight to zero," Sarai chirped, causing me to send her a questioning glare.

Damn, what happened to sisters before misters?

"It's still early, Geffri, don't let him get in your head," she said, reassuringly, "whole lotta ballgame left."

At that I cracked a smile, rolled my shoulders and stepped aside to let Noah take his next turn. Sarai's words were almost like a magic spell, as my luck turned around almost instantaneously, with me making a masterful comeback. By the time we reached the ninth "inning" I was leading Noah by ten "runs".

"Oh," I crowed, cupping a hand near my ear, "Where's all that bragging now? You mighty quiet, Noah Fence. Aye, Rai. What that score looking like?"

He scowled at me using his earlier words against him as both Sarai and Jonah laughed.

"Seventy-four, eighty-four, advantage Robinson," Sarai said, sounding like a scoring judge at Wimbledon.

That just made all of us, including Noah, laugh even harder.

"Yeah, yeah...you know as well as I do that the outcome of this game can change on a dime. So, let's not count our chickens before the eggs hatch, Geffri," Noah said, walking up to take his final turn.

Instead of the confident swagger that he'd maintained for the majority of our games, his steps were measured, almost as if he were mentally calculating if it was really mathematically possible for him to come out with a win on this. Realistically speaking, if he hit all three in this last inning and I missed more than one, he'd emerge the victor. I couldn't let that happen, so I decided to try a distraction tactic of my own, walking right up behind him and softly speaking directly into his ear.

"I guess I also shouldn't remind you that all three of my darts landed in the fifth inning, while you had..." I squinted in the direction of the scoreboard, "exactly one hit? So, my accuracy on that side of the board puts the advantage in my court."

He shrugged me off, "I know what you're trying to do. And it isn't gonna work."

Following up those words with three tosses that landed squarely in the slice of the dartboard for the number nine, then lifted a brow in my direction as to say your move. I skirted around him, taking my place behind the line and trying to do some quick math before I threw my first dart. Since Noah's final score was one hundred and one, I'd only have to hit two darts in the nine spot in order to take the victory. I closed my eyes, took a deep breath, and rolled my shoulders. Opening my eyes, I sent the first dart flying and it easily made its mark. Mentally I celebrated, but outwardly I kept my cool.

"Now," I said, raising my second dart, "If this one hits, I don't even have to throw the third because I'll have won, and you'll be down two games to zero to me."

"Man, get on with it. Nobody asked for this captain obvious ass speech," Noah grumbled.

I threw my second dart, only to have it land a bit too high – sticking firmly in the twelve spot. *Fuck*, I groaned internally.

"Ooh, tough break," Noah jibed, sarcastically, "Would be a shame if you came this far only to lose it all at the end."

I rolled my eyes at him, refocusing on the dart board and throwing as I said, "Nah, I came to embarrass you today and embarrass you is what I shall do."

And as if those words had the power to shift the dart's trajectory, it landed solidly in the nine spot, securing my win! Sarai rushed me with a hug, jumping up and down squealing. Her energy was infectious, I had no choice but to begin jumping along with her.

"I need a drink," Noah grumbled, walking away from where Sarai and I were making a complete fool of ourselves in the middle of a mostly empty bar.

When he came back over with a short glass halfway filled with a dark amber liquid, I quipped, "So...are you willing to admit defeat yet or nah?"

He took a slow sip, his eyes never leaving mine, "We still got a game of pool left, baby girl. Rack 'em."

I grinned, impressed that he wasn't going out easily, but also looking forward to beating his ass at pool too. Growing up, I spent a lot of time at my grandmother's when Pops was working. In grandmother's basement was a pool table – at which I'd spent countless hours as a kid teaching myself how to properly handle a cue and perfecting trick shots. I'd actually earned spending money in undergrad hustling unsuspecting fools at a local pool hall not far from campus.

"Say less," I replied, walking over to the pool table, racking the balls, and grabbing a cue, "we're still on loser leads or..."

Noah drained his drink and then grabbed a cue, nodding his head, "Yep. I'll break."

"Noah, hold up. Remember Will wanted y'all to have a little debrief on camera session after the first two games before you went into the third."

Noah groaned, "I think that was under the assumption that we'd at least be tied up going into this third challenge. Not that I'd be fighting for relevancy at the end here."

"You already know we're gonna hear his shit if you don't though..." Jonah trailed off.

"Ugh, fine," Noah said, raising from where he'd been hunched over to break the balls and leaning against the pool table, cue held upright.

I sidled up next to him, Sarai asking us questions off camera.

"All right y'all, so here we are at the final showdown... thoughts, feelings, emotions at this moment?" she asked, a hint of amusement in her tone.

"I'm feeling good. Feeling great," Noah said sarcastically, before turning toward me, "You?"

I shrugged, "From where I'm standing, he's not too good at nothing, so yanno...*I will not lose.*"

"Oooh, bold claims," Sarai giggled, "Noah, you got any rebuttal?"

"I'd rather be about it, than talk about it," he replied.

"And when I beat you at this game too, will you be about finally admitting that I am better than you or...?"

"You still talkin'...when I already told you," Noah said slyly moving closer to me, "I'm about that action. Say less... let's play, sweetheart."

I looked up at Noah to meet eyes that were clearly filled with desire and I faltered for a second, before recovering.

"L-losers lead, right?" I fumbled over my words.

Noah nodded slowly, a grin stretching across his face before he turned away to go to the end of the table with his cue and commence the last of our games for the evening. I shook off the haze of whatever these currents flowing between us was and paid attention as he broke. It was an excellent break – with Noah sinking the eleven and thirteen balls in opposing corners with the break.

"Stripes it is," he declared with a wink before walking around the perimeter of the table to determine his next shot.

He sank two more balls before finally missing a shot and giving me a chance at the table. I wasted zero time sinking three balls in short order, dusting my shoulders off after every made shot.

"Light work, light work," I said, walking around the table where Noah stood to line up my next shot.

I leaned over the table, then glanced back over my shoulder to talk more shit when I noticed that Noah's eyes were focused squarely on the curve of my ass and not the game at hand. I wasn't the only one who noticed as Sarai tossed a look and giggle my way when she noticed Noah's laser sharp focus.

"Use it," she mouthed, indicating I should use his obvious attraction to my advantage.

I was so out of practice and thrown that Parker's earlier assessment was so spot on, I had no idea how to even do that. I stood upright again, momentarily flustered thinking about having more than Noah's eyes on me.

"I know we've got all night, Robinson, but that doesn't mean you're at liberty to take it," Noah drawled, coming to stand right behind me as he spoke directly into my ear.

I shrugged him off. "You're not scaring anybody, boy," I replied in a tone that was breezier than my building nerves should have allowed, "Just reevaluating my shot."

And with that I moved from where I'd previously been trying to shoot the five ball into a corner pocket, rounding the table and going for a trickier shot that would require me to be damn near laid out on the table, arching my back and tooting my ass more than necessary – trying like hell to "use it" like Sarai had suggested.

"Fuck," I heard Noah expel on a low breath and knew that I'd succeeded.

I ended up missing my shot, but I'd successfully rattled him enough that he missed his next shot as well.

"Time out," Jonah called out, signaling for Noah to come over to where he stood.

"There's no time outs in pool, Jo," Sarai protested, seemingly realizing something that I hadn't picked up on.

They ignored her, huddling together and she hustled over to me.

"Don't lose it," was all she was able to get out before Noah and Jonah broke apart and I set up to take my next turn.

Right as I bent over and situated my cue, Noah came right up behind me, placing one of his hands on my arm that was guiding my shot and the other on the table on the other side of me, effectively boxing me in.

"Your form is terrible," he whispered into my ear, "you won't sink another shot holding your cue like that."

My cue slipped, barely nicking a ball and Noah and Jonah cracked up laughing, slapping high five.

"My turn," Noah said, brushing me aside.

"You…cheater," I said, turning around and getting right in his face, "You purposely distracted me."

"I was just giving you a little advice, Robinson. I have no idea of any of this other mess you are talking about. Now if you'll excuse me," Noah replied calmly, moving his hands in a shooing motion for me to step away from the table.

I narrowed my eyes at him, "Aight bet. You wanna play foul, we can play foul. Sarai, is it warm in here to you?"

She grinned and nodded, "A bit."

"Yeah, me too," I said before removing lightweight, off the shoulder sweatshirt I was wearing over a tank and tying it around my waist, "Ahhhh, much better."

Just as I knew it would, Noah's gaze landed on the low-cut neckline of the longline tank I was wearing, centering in on my titties. To up the ante, I leaned over on the table, damn near spilling out of my top as I goaded Noah.

"I thought you said we don't have all night."

He opened his mouth to say something in reply, but seemingly thought better of it as he stepped back, shook his head and lined up to take his shot again. In rapid succession, he sunk the remaining three balls that he needed to before aiming at the eight ball to win.

"You know," he said while lining up to make his last shot, "as fine as you are, you overestimated how easily I can be distracted."

I was so caught on him thinking I was fine that it barely

registered to me when he sank the eight ball in a corner pocket, winning the game.

"And that, ladies and gentlemen, is what they call game," he said, walking up on the camera that Jonah held, flexing obnoxiously as the both of them cheered.

"Winner on a cheat," I called out.

"The game is the game, baby," Noah shot back, strutting around the pool tables like a peacock, "Gotta keep your focus no matter what. Ain't that the job of an elite pitcher?"

"Whatever you have to tell yourself to justify cheating," I shot back.

"Damn, Robinson, I woulda never pegged you for a sore loser."

"And I never would have thought you'd cheat to win, so I guess we're both learning something new today," I shrugged.

"She's right, Noah," Sarai tried to reason, "You totally cheated when you were all up on her ass. Elite pitchers don't have folks putting dicks on their lower back as distraction."

At that comment Jonah spit out the sip of beer he'd just taken.

"Fine, rack 'em again and I'll hand Geffri her ass *once again*. Easily."

"No dickstractions this time?" Sarai pressed and I blushed, waving her off.

I shook my head. "Nah, fool me once…"

"C'mon Geffri. You got this, girl!" Sarai insisted.

I shook my head once again. "I'll take my legit wins, but I ain't setting myself up for the okie doke again with this guy."

"Awwww don't be like that, Robinson. Desperate times call for desperate measures, I had to do what I had to do. I couldn't go out, shut out."

I rolled my eyes, "Whatever, man."

"Lemme make it up to you," Noah said, moving closer to me.

I sidestepped him, untying my sweatshirt from my waist and dragging it over my head, "I'm good."

Noah stepped in my path once again, gazing down on me with that same lust-filled look from earlier. "You sure?" he asked in a low growl.

And suddenly I wasn't so sure at all. Especially when he lowered his head and whispered into my ear, "All bullshit aside, Geffri, I'ma just keep it straight with you. I am *very* interested in getting to know you a bit better. And if you'll let me, I'd like to...properly make amends for pulling an underhanded trick to escape being pegged a loser. So whaddya say?" His lips grazed my ear as he whispered his impassioned plea. That simple contact and the charge of electricity it brought with was enough to get me to change my mind.

Biting down on my lower lip, I gazed up at him through with what I was sure was a heated look in my eyes and asked, "What did you have in mind?"

Moments later after we'd separated from Jonah and Sarai, I found myself in a surprisingly spacious apartment above *Smitty's* sitting on an *IKEA* couch waiting for Noah to return with an *Angry Orchard* cider for me. He invited me up to his place so we could talk, beyond the confines of our little competition and get to know one another without the presence of those pesky cameras. Since I was intrigued, and attracted, I submitted, but once we got up here my nerves from earlier in the day reappeared. I didn't know what the hell I was thinking following this man – *that I barely knew –* up to his apartment, *alone*. I didn't get any vibes from Noah that made me think that I should be on guard, but I was still way out of my element here.

Noah reappeared in the living room and I bit my lip to keep from crying out at the change in his attire. He'd been dressed simply earlier, in jeans and a crisp white tee that showcased his impressive upper body and arms, but he traded that for a more comfy casual pair of ball shorts and a black, ribbed tank that molded to his form so perfectly that I could count every damned ab muscle that he possessed. It barely registered to me that he'd been holding out my requested drink in my direction until he sat down next to me on the couch and called out my name. It was then that I shook out of the haze I'd been in to accept the drink, greedily drinking nearly the entire bottle in one sip – I was *that damned thirsty*. In more ways than one.

"Whoa, slow down, killa. There's no rush," Noah cracked, and I giggled nervously in response.

As our laughter died down, Noah remained quiet, staring at me in an almost unnerving way. I turned my head toward the television where he'd turned it to some random collegiate football game that I couldn't give two shits about when I heard him murmur, "You know you really are beautiful, Geffri."

He followed those words with a hand lightly trailing up my arm, across my collarbone, to settle upon the nape of my neck as he turned me to face him. I remained silent, drinking in his handsome toasted almond colored face – thick, sandy brown brows framed expressive hazel eyes that darkened and lightened depending upon his mood, a broad, Nubian nose situated atop thick, rosy colored lips, shadowed by a light, sandy beard that appeared to be less of a purposeful growing of facial hair, but the side effect of skipping the razor for a few days in a row. He was an incredibly beautiful man…who was currently staring at me like the secrets of the universe were somewhere in the depths of my eyes. I hadn't noticed it earlier, but now that I was unabashedly staring, I peeped the lightest smattering of freckles across the bridge of his nose, resembling some sort of Milky Way borne constellation.

"You know who you look like?" Noah said suddenly.

I groaned, already knowing what he was going to say. Ever since I'd started letting my hair grow out longer, I'd gotten the same celebrity comparison. She was a cute girl, so I wasn't mad about it, but since I was older than her folks steadily saying I looked like Zendaya felt like a slight at times. Like, damn, I was here on earth first, she was just more well known. A silly thing to quibble about but quibbling about silly shit was one of my favorite pastimes.

"Let me guess...Zendaya," I sighed.

Noah squinted at me and tilted his head, "I mean...I guess I can see that, too, but that's not who I was going to say."

Now he had me curious because I'd been hearing this Zendaya thing for the past two years, but prior to that had never had anyone compare me to any other celebrity.

"Who...were you going to say?" I asked, softly.

"You remember that show *Everybody Hates Chris*? You look like...Tasha."

I narrowed my eyes, trying to recall what she looked like in my head, but coming up blank.

"I...don't know if that's a compliment or what. I can't call her to mind in my head."

Noah leaned in a bit, getting right up in my face as he said, "Oh it's *most definitely* a compliment. I had the *biggest* crush on her back in the day."

"That's why you wanna get to know me? Because I look like your childhood crush?" I frowned.

Noah shook his head. "I wanna get to know you because you beat my ass handily at games that I normally kill at. You got a smart-ass mouth with the skills to back it up. *And, you fine as hell.*"

He ended his little speech with a quick flick of his tongue across my lower lip that should have been a turn off, but instead ignited a dormant fire within me. We went from staring and sharing air to me launching myself forward into his lap, tangling my hands in his soft curls and attacking his mouth with gusto. If Noah was taken aback by my sudden action, he took it all in stride, settling his hands at my waist and tangling his tongue with mine as I ground against his burgeoning erection. Disengaging our mouths, his trailed his mouth down to my neck, where he nipped and suckled my skin hard enough to leave marks, but I didn't care as long as he didn't stop doing what he was doing. He dragged his hands from my waist upward, the pads of his fingers gently sliding up my abdomen as his thumbs softly grazed the underside of my titties, making me arch into him. I moaned as his hot hands covered my titties fully, squeezing softly.

At the sound of my moan, Noah pulled back slowly, staring at me again with his lip pulled between his damned teeth.

"My bad, I…didn't invite you up here for *this*," he apologized, sliding his hands from where they'd been under my shirt back down to my waist, trying to move me from his lap.

I placed my hands atop his and shook my head.

"What would you say if I told you that *this* is *exactly* what I came up here for though?" I countered, bringing forth a surprised gleam in Noah's eyes.

"Look," I said, guiding his hands right back to cup my titties, "this thing between us has been brewing all day. And instead of ignoring it, like logical Geffri would do, I'm embracing it and going with the flow."

Noah threw his head back and groaned as I manipulated his hands to give my tits another tight squeeze.

"I'm trying to practice restraint, Robinson," he gritted out as I leaned down and ran my tongue along the side of his neck before snagging his earlobe between my teeth.

"Fuck your restraint. The fact of the matter is I want you, Noah. So why won't you let me have you?" I crooned.

With those words, he stood, wrapping my long legs

around his waist as he guided us from the living room back to his bedroom, promptly depositing me on the bed. I grinned at the heated look in his eye, knowing that whatever he was going to bring I was more than ready for. This entire day had been one long foreplay session, with us upping the ante at each encounter bringing us closer and closer to this moment. He stripped out of his tank and shorts quickly, leaving himself clad in just his boxers as he moved toward where I laid on my back on the bed, perched on my elbows taking in the view. Soon he had me in a similar state of undress, clad only in my bra and panties – *which were matching today, thankfully* – kissing a deliberate path from where he'd just yanked my jeggings from my feet all the way back up to my mouth. Our tongues dueled as our hands explored, acquainting ourselves with the hills and valleys of our bodies, committing the landscapes to memory.

Soon though, the kissing wasn't enough, and I was ready to round a few more bases – communicating my desire by slipping my hands into Noah's boxers and slowly caressing his "bat". He wasn't even completely hard, yet my hand could barely wrap around his dick fully. My action garnered the exact reaction I expected as he groaned and commenced to stripping me out of my underwear before shedding his own and reaching over to grab a condom out of the nightstand. I reached to grab it from his hand, wanting to do the honors of rolling it onto his tumescent hardness, but he tossed it onto the top of the nightstand and shook his head.

"Nah, not yet," he gritted out.

I groaned in discontent, wishing he'd stop playing with me and get to it, but before I could verbalize a complaint, Noah leaned down to capture one of my nipples in his mouth, rolling his tongue around it as it stiffened at the stimulation. Just like that any of my irritation was melted away as he used his mouth all over my exposed skin, licking, sucking, nibbling, and nipping his way to my center where he dove in face first, spreading me open and worshiping me with his mouth like he'd found a new religion. I squealed and squirmed as he went after me relentlessly putting his tongue in places that'd been previously untouched – every lap sending me careening toward release.

"Noah, please," I beseeched, not knowing exactly what I was begging for, but hoping he could interpret it to assuage my needs.

My pleas just made him go even harder, flickering his tongue against my swollen pearl as he added his fingers to the party, sliding deftly through my wetness, ratcheting my desire to fever pitch and when he crooked them in a slight come here motion, that was enough to send me completely over the edge. I came with a sharp cry, arching from the bed and grasping his forearm to keep his fingers exactly where they were as I came in a shuddering mess of quivers. Prolonging my orgasm beyond what I thought was humanly possibly was clearly Noah's goal as he continued the ministrations of his fingers within my pussy while kissing his way back up to my face that held a stupefied expression of bliss. He kissed me in tandem with the movements of his fingers, slow and methodical, content to drive me out of my mind without even the thought of penile penetration. He kissed me with zero sense of urgency, with long, languid strokes of his tongue against mine before pulling back to nibble at my lips.

I'd finally come back to myself enough to put my hands to good use as I trailed them down the front of his body until I reached the treasure that I sought. Wrapping as much of my hand as I could around his thick – *and now fully erect* – dick, I stroked him once, twice just as slowly as his fingers worked me, drawing a moan from him that just spurred me on. With my other hand, I slowly withdrew his fingers from my center, maneuvering to run the head of his dick along my slickened entrance.

"*Shit*," Noah groaned before moving back, grabbing the condom, quickly sheathing himself and slamming into me.

He slow stroked me, drawing whimper after moan out of me as he plummeted my depths before flipping us over, settling his back against the headboard.

With a slap to my ass, he urged, "Ride it."

I needed no further instruction as I rolled my hips against him in a fluid motion, giddy from the sounds that left his mouth with each movement of my body. He kept his hands planted on my waist as he guided my motion, stroking upward on my every downswing. Unable to continue at the maddeningly slow pace for too long, I switched it up, balancing my weight on my feet as I bounced up on down on his dick rapidly, drawing another of those lowly grumbled curses from Noah's mouth as he gave up on trying to control the tempo and let me go crazy on his dick, bringing us both to a gratifying explosion of passion. I slumped onto his body, completely wrung out, as he wrapped his arms around me tightly, drawing abstract shapes on my back with his fingers as we both came down from the high.

SIXTH INNING

*J*didn't remember falling asleep, but as I awakened no longer sprawled atop Noah, but casually tucked into his side I couldn't help the grin that spread across my face. That didn't last long as the memories of throwing myself at Noah like some sort of desperate floozy set in and I felt super embarrassed by my actions. I knew that he was feeling me, but I'd never done anything like this before, usually preferring to let the guy finally make the move. I dunno what emboldened me, but now in the light of day...well technically it was still the cover of dark since according to the clock on Noah's dresser it was three forty-seven am...I was feeling all out of sorts. Tentatively, I lifted my head from where it rested on Noah's outstretched arm, turning as gingerly as I possibly could as to not cause him to stir awake. Taking in his face brought another unbidden grin to my face. *Talking about I'm fine as hell, nah you the fine one* I thought as I shifted to sit up in bed. I gave my eyes a second to adjust to the darkness of the room before I attempted to gather my belongings and get my ass outta dodge before Noah woke up. My feet had just hit the ground and I was about to stand up when Noah spoke up.

"Wow, were you gonna leave money on the nightstand or just skate on me like a thief in the night?"

I flinched hard, damn near leaping to the ceiling at the sound of his voice.

Turning around I gasped, "You just scared the shit out of me!"

Noah sat up on his side of the bed, getting out and coming around to hold me in a loose embrace. He buried his face in my neck, nipping at my skin before speaking.

"Damn, did I not show you a good enough time last night? Felt like you needed to sneak out under the cover of darkness so no one would see where you were coming from? Cold world..."

I groaned, then laughed. "Shut up, Noah. That's not it at a-all."

Definitely not it I thought as he moved his mouth to kiss behind my ear. Quite the opposite in fact. I'd had an amazing time with him last night and didn't want it to end.

"Okay, so what is it?"

"I have a lot to do today before I take off, is all," I whined as his tongue glided along the curve of my collarbone.

I stepped back, out of his embrace, and I tried to continue getting dressed, but Noah's hands at my waist stopped me once again.

"Geffri," he said, placing a hand under my chin to bring my gaze to his, "it's four in the morning. What, pray tell, do you have to do that's so important that you had to skulk outta my house this early ruining my plans for early morning cuddling and fondling before I made you the one good thing I can cook – *a cheese omelet* – and then let you get on with your day."

"I'm lactose intolerant," I said, stupidly.

"Is...that all you took from that?" Noah chuckled, then let me go, "Wow, okay I can take a hint."

"Wait...I'm not hinting at...," I groaned, "Sorry, I'm just...I don't have much experience at...this."

"This?" he queried.

"Post one night stand etiquette," I offered with a shrug.

Noah held up his hands. "Whoa, who said this was a one night *anything?*"

I shrugged again, mumbling about not knowing what the hell any of this was and he pulled me back into an embrace, keeping me flush against him.

"I meant it when I said I wanted to get to know you, Geffri. That wasn't me running game to get you up here to fuck you. I find you...intriguing. So, let's talk about how we can get to know one another better."

"Right now?"

"You got somewhere else you need to be?"

I shook my head and let him lead me back to his bed where we settled beneath the covers with him spooning me. I couldn't front, I was incredibly pleased with this turn of events despite having no idea what the hell I was getting myself into. We laid in silence for a few minutes before Noah's hands began to wander, making good on that early morning fondling he'd spoken of earlier. I moaned as his hand trailed down the outside of my thigh before settling between my legs to play in the wetness that'd blossomed as he convinced me to stay a while. With slow, sloppy kisses on my neck and my clit pinched between his thumb and forefinger, Noah had me panting in no time, clawing at him as I begged for release. The devious chuckle that came from him as he continued to strum me like an instrument did nothing to quell the sensations that ricocheted through me when he'd finally put me out of my misery and hooked his fingers inside my pussy, pressing down on a spot that made me cum instantaneously.

I didn't even remember falling asleep again but awakened to the smell of bacon wafting into the room. I dragged myself outta Noah's bed, snagged his discarded shirt from last night and padded out to find the source of the smell. As I rounded the corner to the kitchen, I could hear Noah singing along with the music that was softly playing in the kitchen. He actually didn't have a bad tone or maybe I was still in the post-orgasm haze where he was able to do no wrong.

"Good morning," I rasped as I walked up to where he stood in front of the stove, flipping an omelet.

He turned and drew me into him, pressing a quick kiss to my forehead. "Hey, Sleeping Beauty, bout time you got up."

"Shut up," I groaned, laughing, "Smells good in here though."

"Sit down," he said, nudging me in the direction of the table that was already set with glasses and juice and water alongside silverware.

I didn't have to bet told twice and moments later he was walking our breakfast over to the table.

"Bon appetite."

He'd paid attention to my early morning lactose commentary because instead of an omelet like he had, my plate had fluffy scrambled eggs, a couple strips of bacon and two pieces of toast. I thanked him as I grabbed my plate from him, waiting for him to sit down before I grabbed his hands to say a quick grace. If he was surprised, he didn't let it show, just echoed my amen at the end of the quick prayer and tucked into eating. Despite him saying that he only knew how to cook one thing well, breakfast was delicious. After we ate, Noah finally let me get dressed and provided me a toothbrush so I could at least clean my mouth before I headed out for my day but promised to reach out to me later, so we could continue *getting to know each other.*

"You don't even have my phone number."

"I don't need it."

"How do you suppose we're going to communicate while I'm gone then?"

"I can just slide in your DM. Worked like a charm the first time," Noah smirked, "Or I can just hit that FaceTime request and ask you to let me watch you play with that pretty pussy of yours, keeping it warm for me 'til you make it back home."

I laughed, "You are just..."

"Irresistible?" Noah supplied, "Yeah, I know..."

"You really just say whatever the hell comes to mind, huh?"

"Don't front like you don't enjoy it."

"Anyway...I've got to go. Got a flight to catch in," I peered over his shoulder to look at the clock, "just over six hours and I haven't packed a solitary thing. And I have a lunch thing with my Pops and his girlfriend."

"You don't have to explain your hurry to bounce up outta here to me," Noah cracked, "Just glad you let me feed you before you left. Can't have my hospitality out here in question in the streets."

I sidled up to him, pressing a quick kiss against his closed mouth. "Trust me, you have been way more than hospitable."

Noah deepened the kiss, allowing our tongues to play before he pulled back with a loud smack to my ass. "Another happy customer, make sure you leave a five-star review on Yelp."

I just rolled my eyes, gathering my things to walk out of the door.

"Later, Noah."

"Eagerly awaiting the next time, Geffri."

After I left Noah's I headed straight home to shower and

SIXTH INNING • 77

relax a little while before I headed over to my dad's to have lunch with him and Brenda. I planned on packing so I could just have Pops drop me off at the airport after I was done hanging out with the two of them. Even though my flight wasn't until after five this evening, I had a serious phobia of missing my flight due to TSA lines, so I always ended up at the airport way earlier than necessary as a precautionary measure. When I got to Pops', I made sure to knock before entering the house using my key. Despite him and Miss Brenda knowing I was coming; I didn't want to walk in on any *afternoon delight*. I walked into the house to see the two of them in the kitchen, in their own little world, swaying together while Al Green's "Simply Beautiful" played in the background. It was cute—seeing Pops in this way with a woman. Something I'd never witnessed in all of my years on earth, a sweet moment I almost hated to break up by announcing my presence. So, I backpedaled back to the front of the house, calling out a greeting.

"In the kitchen, Speedy," Pops called out.

He'd just pulled the lasagna out of the oven, so I had perfect timing. As soon as I crossed over into the kitchen, Miss Brenda greeted me with what I would soon learn was one of her signature hugs. We sat down, dished up the food and I kicked off the conversation with a question I knew would throw Pops for a loop, but was something that I was curious about.

"How did you guys meet?"

They shared an amused look as they went back and forth about who would tell the story before deciding that Miss Brenda was the one who should tell it.

"Well, Leon and I have known each other for years, actually," she started, before launching into the story of them meeting because they both walked out of a group for grieving widow and widowers after finding out that the leader of the group was using their stories for fodder in a collection of creative non-fiction essays that he'd eventually publish. The day they left the group, it was a handful of them – about five or six people, who'd all decided to form their own subgroup. Over the years, the group waned, but Pops and Miss Brenda stayed in touch – strictly platonic.

"Until one day, she couldn't resist ya old Pops," my dad broke in, causing Miss Brenda to giggle and defer to him to tell the rest of the story. According to Pops she used to make excuses to have him over to her house to fix things that were broken – a leaky faucet here, a broken dryer there, but he didn't mind it at all because he was feeling her the whole time too. They thankfully left out the details of the transition from platonic to more than…but I'd gotten the gist of it all. And they were adorable as hell, finishing each other's sentences as they shared the tale with me.

"Now Speedy, when is your first exhibition game? I ain't missed too many of your games and I won't start now. Bren's never been to Texas, so I told her we can come down there and check you out."

"Admittedly, I don't know much about baseball, much to your father's chagrin, but I'd love to see you in action, Geffri."

"It'd be dope if you guys could come down to see a game," I grinned, "Blair and Parker are trying to work out something to come check out a game or two as well. We're playing exhibition games against some local teams starting on the fifteenth. I can text you the exact details so y'all can make plans, if it works for your schedules."

"We'll make it work for our schedules, ain't that right, baby?" Pops crooned.

Miss Brenda just nodded and grinned in agreement. After we were done eating and had sat around talking a little longer, it was time for me to get to the airport. Pops had fallen asleep in his favorite recliner and Miss Brenda insisted that we didn't need to wake him, that she could just drop me off. I knew he'd feel a way, though, if I didn't at least attempt to wake him before I got up out of there, so I nudged him awake, gave him a hug and kiss, and amidst his complaints, followed Miss Brenda out to her car so she could drop me off before finishing up her errands. The ride to the airport was quick and uneventful, as was the TSA line, so I had a smooth two hours to waste before boarding for my flight would even begin. I figured I'd call the girls to catch them up on the latest developments in my life. I shot them both a text to make sure they could actually talk right now before sending a group FaceTime invite. Once we were all connected it took Blair no time to call me out.

"Oh bih, you got a glow," she squealed in lieu of a greeting.

I could feel my face reddening as she kept going on and on about how I looked so refreshed and rejuvenated.

"It ain't just being on the cusp of actualizing one of your childhood dreams either," Blair continued.

"Sure isn't!" Parker chimed in with a sly chuckle, "How'd the rest of yesterday go, G?"

"Oh…I lost the pool game," I said, trying to remain nonchalant but the memories of how the rest of the night progressed after Noah and mine's little showdown put a silly ass grin across my face.

Blair, ever the observant one, whispered, "Holy shit. You little slut! You banged the troll? I'm so proud of youuuuu."

"I…" I started.

"It's all over your face, sis," Blair continued, as she narrowed her eyes and pulled her phone closer to her face, "And…your neck. Lil buddy went to town on you, huhn?"

"Blair, please," Parker broke in, "let Geffri fill us in on the nitty gritty. Actually, wait…lemme pour me a glass of wine for this one."

"Isn't it a little early for wine, sis?" I asked.

"It's five o'clock somewhere. And I ain't on the clock," Parker replied, with a shrug.

"And, you're stalling," Blair said, "how'd you get from teaching dude a lesson to him showing you how your pussy works?"

I nearly spit out the sip of ginger ale I'd just taken, my effort to keep it in my mouth sent some of it flying up my nose.

"I swear I cannot stand your ass, Blair," I said, once I'd recovered, "I don't need anyone to show me that, by the way. Me and my five friends do *just fine* – shout out to Auntie Mary J – figuring that out."

"Oh God," Parker said, with a hand to her forehead, "That part we didn't ever need to know."

"At the fuck all," Blair chimed in.

"You have no one to blame but yourself, BlairBear," I grinned, "But nah, seriously…all bullshit aside, we ended up hanging out a bit after the little competition aspect of our day was over and despite being a troll online, Noah is actually a really cool dude. Super sweet. Said he was interested in getting to know me better and I couldn't front like I wasn't curious about him too, especially after my Google sleuthing. The attraction between us was mutual, as PDiddy already pointed out. One thing led to another and…"

"You tripped and fell on his dick!" Blair finished for me.

"Well, not exactly, but I did make the first move," I blushed.

"You did?" they both screeched in unison before we all broke out into giggles.

"Yes! Sometimes I go for what I want in life," I protested.

"When it comes to professional endeavors, you *absolutely do*," Blair reasoned, "But with *men*? You? Geffri Denise Robinson? Never experienced that emotion. Hell, I only need one hand…nay, one finger to run down the times you've actually made a real first move. And that would be referencing this one time you just told us about right now. Oh, he must be *fine* fine."

"He's a little…too light for you," Parker tossed out, referencing Blair's affinity for blue-black brothers, "but he really is handsome. Hell, I thought G was gonna mount him in the park, honestly."

"Oh, shut up, Stepmom!" I cracked.

Blair and I broke into giggles, but Parker's face suddenly got super serious like she'd seen a ghost before she mumbled that she'd call us back. I had no idea what that was about, but Blair and I kept talking for a few minutes more. I didn't give her the nitty gritty of everything that'd happened between Noah and me, but I told her enough that she felt compelled to share how happy she was for me and how she hoped that this thing between he and I turned into something. Truthfully, I was out of my depth here and hoped for the same. I couldn't let myself get too caught up in thinking about that for now though because I had a more pressing mission to complete over the next few weeks.

SEVENTH INNING

By the time I got to Texas, it was after ten pm since my flight had a layover that turned into a delayed second flight. I was told that my arrival time wouldn't be an issue since there was someone who would be working the front desk of the dorms we'd be occupying on the college campus where we'd be playing and practicing before traveling to Toronto for the international tournament that we'd be playing in. I was overtired and ready to face plant, so I was grateful that my check-in process was swift, and it took less than five minutes from the time I left my Lyft to make my way to my room. I was relieved to open the door to a dark and empty room. I wouldn't be blessed with a solo room, the sign on the door welcoming me – *and someone named Keni* – quashed those thoughts, but at least I'd beat the girl I would be rooming with to town and could set myself up how I wanted before she arrived. I knew nothing of most of the folks on this team beyond the fact that I'd likely be on the older end of the roster. It was cool though, I kind of liked the idea of being a veteran player in age, but a rookie in experience as far as playing on this stage. I unpacked quickly, took a quick shower to wash the plane germs off me, switched out the sheets that were provided on the bed, then climbed between my newly purchased sheets and slid headfirst into slumberland.

When I woke up the next morning, my phone's screen was full of texts and missed calls since I'd forgotten to let my people know that I'd arrived safely. I was entirely too concerned with laying my ass down, so that was my bad, but I started with Pops, giving him a quick call to let him know that I'd made it and then made my way down the line to my grandmother and then my friends so that they could stop cussing me out in their minds with each hour that passed and I didn't reply to their attempts to reach me. According to the schedule, I wasn't expected to meet up with the rest of the team, coaches, and other staff until around noon, so I decided to Yelp my way into a delicious breakfast before I had to get into training mode. I ended up at a cute little coffee shop that was advertised as having the best cup of coffee and quiche in the contiguous United States. I don't know what I was expecting when I walked into a place that looked straight out of a Hallmark movie about a high-powered executive who left behind their life of stress in the big city to follow their heart and open up a small town bakery, but it definitely was not finding a sista at the center of it all. I wasn't mad at it all though, positively thrilled to be able to support a small Black business while getting my grub on.

This morning as I got ready for the day, I'd noticed that I left a few key items at home in my hasty packing, so after breakfast I went to Target before traveling back to the dorms. This time, when I arrived back to my room, the sound of music with a pulsing, rhythmic beat was blaring. I stifled a giggle at my roomie, I assumed, with her eyes closed, hands in the air, getting down as she unpacked her clothing –

fully lost in the music. I cleared my throat loudly, which made her jump before she grabbed her phone to turn the music off and then turned in my direction.

"You scared the stuffing out of me! Hi!"

"Keni?" I ventured, pronouncing it like the shortened version of Kenneth, "You were getting down, girl. I almost hated to disturb your groove."

She shook her head. "Key-Knee," she corrected, "It's Ghanaian. And I'm not even gonna attempt to pronounce your name because in my brain I'm pronouncing it with a hard g, but in my heart that feels wrong."

I laughed loudly. "It's a soft g. Like the giraffe from Toys 'R Us."

Keni's nose scrunched in confusion at my reference and I shook my head. "The butler from Fresh Prince?"

"Okay, okay, now I feel you. Nice to meet you," she gushed, pulling me into a hug, "I'm a hugger. You don't mind, do you?"

"If I did, it'd be too late now, huh?" I cracked.

"Touché," Keni replied disengaging from our embrace.

"You're good," I laughed, lest she get the wrong impression, "But hey...turn that music back up though, it was jamming. Reminds me of *The Gift*."

"Yeah, y'alls girl did borrow quite a bit from my people for that album," Keni quipped.

I held up my hands, "Aye, I'm not tryna start diaspora wars outchea. That's my only frame of reference is all."

Keni giggled, "I'm just so used to giving my friends who are fans of the Queen Bey shit. I've got no real beef, honestly. I love that she actually collaborated with artists from the continent instead of Columbusing our shit like some others though."

I nodded, not knowing what else to say to that, instead choosing to switch the topic of our conversation.

"So, what position do you play?" I asked.

"A little of everything, honestly. But I'm hoping to make it out of the exhibition stage of this as our team's catcher. That's the role I played on my university softball team for the past four years and it's where I've grown most comfortable."

"Makes sense why they paired us as roomies then."

"You're a hurler?" Keni grinned.

"Guilty as charged."

"Righty or southpaw?"

"Both."

She whistled and nodded her head in approval.

"Oh, so you being a part of this team is kind of a foregone conclusion, huh?"

"Prayerfully," I replied, not giving any indication that I had any insider information. As far as she knew, I was just like her – here for the exhibition and hopeful for a spot on the final roster.

"Can I tell you how happy I was to see you as my roommate though? I have never played with another Black girl on my team, so this feels like some unicorn melanin mami magique shit," I cracked, causing Keni to laugh as well.

"Growing up my brothers were all sports fanatics and being born smack dab in the middle of five, I had to either adapt or be left behind. I played softball too, but when this opportunity came my way? I had to give it a go. Baseball has a special place in my heart, it was my paternal grandfather's favorite sport and I spent countless hours watching it with him growing up. He never played the sport, but that didn't deaden his passion, you know?"

I nodded. "Yeah, growing up with my Pops who forwent his opportunity to take his ball playing to the next level I always felt like I had a responsibility to take it as far as I could. He's actually the reason I'm here. He was insistent on me giving this a whirl before I completely hung up my glove and fully committed to coaching."

"Well I guess we gotta go out there and give it our all, huh? Make a name for ourselves and ensure that we secure the bag."

"Yep. Let's make sure we're paired together as often as possible, so we can each make the other look good."

"That's a bet," Keni eagerly agreed.

"How long have you been here? Have you gotten a chance to go stomp in the dirt yet?"

She shook her head. "I'd literally just got here minutes before you walked in. Flicking up her wrist to look at the smart watch that was on it, she continued, "It's just about that time for us to be headed over to meet up with everyone though. Gimme a couple minutes to change and we can walk over together?"

"Sounds like a plan," I said, sprawling across my bed as Keni moved to swap out the cute little dress she was wearing for some athleisure wear.

I was already dressed in workout leggings and a tee, so I wouldn't have to change when I returned from my morning errands. As I laid there waiting for Keni to be ready, my phone pinged with a notification from Twitter, I swiped it to see that it was Noah, sliding in my DMs like he'd promised. And he'd literally slid in, dropping a gif of Frankie Lindor sliding into second in my inbox. I couldn't even help the giggle that escaped my mouth after I let the gif loop a couple times.

"Silly ass," I muttered as I typed out a simple reply of "hey".

@noahhhfence312: just wanted to wish you luck on your first day, but as your trouncing of me a few days ago proved, your natural talent outweighs luck any day. Strike 'em all out, killa. The whole town.

I laughed again, not really certain that I'dve pegged him for being this silly. I typed out a quick thanks in reply, still shaking my head and laughing as Keni returned.

"Uttt, I know the sound of that kinda giggle," Keni said, stepping back into the room, "Am I interrupting bae time?"

I shot up, stowing my phone, and shaking my head.

"Not at all, chica. You ready?"

"Yep."

The dorm we were in was about ten minutes from the athletic center and Keni and I took the time to get to know each other even further. She was semi-local, a homegrown Texas girl, though from a city about four hours from where we were currently stationed. She was three years younger than me, and engaged to her high school sweetheart, who was a professional soccer player. On the walk over she kept remarking how I looked familiar, but she couldn't place it. I certainly was not going to even try to figure out from where or why she thought she knew me, so I just insisted that I must have one of those faces. Because I swear if this girl told me I looked like *KC Undercover* our newfound friendship would be sinking instantaneously. We were among the first to arrive to the field, greeting Ray and the rest of the crew as others slowly trickled in.

It was a little awkward at first once everyone gathered because they made us all go around and introduce ourselves with a silly little ice breaker before we got down to brass tax and began working out and doing drills. The time that we were scheduled to be out there past quickly, over before I really felt like I'd hit my stride. It was fun, being back in a team environment, but slightly different because there was less of the having to prove myself element of it. Whenever I played with guys, I always felt like I had to come in with a sign around my neck that said "yes, I am a girl and yes I can strike you the fuck out". Here the edge of competition was there, but not in a way where I felt consistently compelled to prove my talent. I honestly think that meeting with the Team USA representatives in advance of this minicamp helped with that.

The first day went by pretty quickly, with us only being out there practicing for just over ninety minutes and then having the rest of the day free. Ray let everyone know that we'd be split into four groups of ten, rotating players from group to group daily to get a feel for chemistry. We'd have practice in the mornings – two hours – then a few hours of time to ourselves for lunch and whatever else we decided to get into before evening intramural games amongst ourselves. During practice and these games, our every move would be scrutinized – with the Team USA reps looking not only for the most skilled players, but for the ones who would also bring a certain level of commitment and chemistry to the final twenty-woman squad. Ray had a handful of assistant coaches at his disposal who, along with the general manager and program director, would have the final say so for the squad that'd eventually travel to Toronto to compete.

On our walk back, Keni's mouth ran a mile a minute talking about everything from the coaching staff to the other girls, nothing malicious just giving all of her observations. I learned fairly quickly that girl was a talker and I just let her go, chiming in with appropriate sounds of assent dotted with the occasional Willow Smithesque "Mmmmhmmm". No sooner than we'd made it back to the room, Keni dipped out, going off to hang out with one of her undergrad teammates who was a local. I was glad for the reprieve, pulling out my computer to watch some *Schitt's Creek* on *Netflix*. Parker was obsessed with this show and I told her I'd give it a shot. I was glad she'd suggested it because half an episode in I was cracking up and wishing I'd grabbed some wine or something from Target to drink along with my bingeing. I was three episodes into season one when the FaceTime chime interrupted my viewing. At the sight of Noah's name, I grinned, but quickly schooled my features into a more neutral expression when I connected the call.

"You do know that an unscheduled FaceTime call is equivalent to just showing up to someone's house uninvited, right?" I asked in lieu of greeting.

Noah just grinned at me. "But you answered though."

I couldn't say anything smart in reply because he'd gotten me. Not only had I answered, but the tone had barely gotten through an entire cycle before I tapped the little green button on the touch bar of my MacBook. *Too thirsty to see his handsome ass face*, I mentally chided myself.

"That I did."

"So, how's it going?"

"Well, so far. I mean we've only had a brief practice so far, so it hasn't been too much to really…assess, you know? I haven't gotten to know anyone, but my roommate and we haven't gotten any games in. How are things with you?"

"Man," Noah heaved a sigh, "pretty tough if I'm being honest."

Concern creased my forehead as I replied, "Oh yeah, what's going on…if you don't mind me asking?"

"It's wild, right?' he started, before trailing off and looking away from his camera, then dramatically turning back to face me, "A couple weeks ago I was trolling this athlete on Twitter, right? Then I ended up challenging her to a competition and she beat my ass *handily*, while looking *sexy as hell* the whole time, so I had to shoot my shot at her right? And she went for it. Which is no shock, because look at me, right? A nigga is handsome as hell. But then she had to leave town before we could really start fucking with each other. So, I been sitting here trying not to be too thirsty and accidentally double tap any photos as I scrolled back one hundred ninety-six weeks in her Instagram. Plus, the rules dictated that I needed to wait the prerequisite couple of days to contact her, so I looked less pressed, right?"

I just nodded, biting my lower lip to keep my laughter at bay. I just wanted to see how far he would go with this.

"Then I remembered that I didn't need to worry about coming off as pressed because she consented to letting me FaceTime her to watch her play with her pussy whenever I wanted to and…"

"I did not consent to that!" I shrieked while simultaneously laughing.

"Are you sure?" Noah asked, his face tilted upward with a finger on his chin, "Because I definitely remember putting that option on the table and you didn't take it off. So, I assumed that meant you'd be into takin' it off on camera for ya boy? Did I…read that wrong?"

"I am not playing with myself on camera for you, Noah. I have a whole roommate over here."

"And you're having this conversation without any headphones in? Okay, Geffri's an exhibitionist," he murmured, pretending to take notes with a pen and pad in front of him.

"Oh my God, you are a mess," I giggled, "My roommate isn't here right now."

"Perfect, that means you can…"

I shook my head, "Do nothing but have a conversation with you, *still*."

"Damn, okay can we negotiate? A brotha can't see a nipple? A peench of areola?"

I had no reply but my uncontrollable laughter.

"Ok, fine. Live action viewing is off the table, but how about stills? I mean I probably have enough in my mental spank bank to last for at least the first week you're gone, but after that I may need some supplemental material."

"Noah! Oh my God!" I groaned, covering my face with my hands, but still laughing my ass off at his silliness.

"*Fine*," he continued, "Guess I'll just have to hold off until...*never mind.*"

"Until when?" I asked, interest piqued.

"Sorry, it's classified information," Noah replied with a straight face.

I shook my head, laughing at him again.

"Silly ass. How was *your* day for real?" I asked.

"Pretty dope, honestly. Got back the revisions on my article from an editor I've been waiting to hear back from, and he only wanted a couple changes, which was pretty dope because he's usually on my ass about every little thing. Secured an interview with a descendant of a Negro Leagues player for the podcast on *b&b*, and now I'm sitting here looking at your pretty face. Cherry on a perfect sundae of a day."

"Flatterer."

"Truthteller in the Lord's Army is all I am, sweetheart," he replied smoothly.

We chatted a bit longer about nothing particularly earth shattering until Keni returned. I ended our call because I couldn't find my headphones and I didn't want my roommate all in my business. I got up to take a quick shower before settling into bed for the night and when I returned, Keni snapped her fingers and pointed at me.

"Oh! I meant to tell you. At dinner we figured out why you looked so familiar to me."

"Oh yeah?" I asked, walking past her to slide into my bed.

She nodded once. "Anyone ever told you that you look like Zendaya?"

I groaned, throwing my pillow over my head.

"What? She's *gorgeous*!" Keni said, "Like, that's a universal truth, right?"

"She absolutely is, but if anything, *she* looks like *me*. I was here first! Y'all gotta put some respeck on my age!" I laughed.

Keni shook her head at me. "A mess. But I'm glad I figured it out. It was gonna mess with me this whole time if I couldn't figure it out."

"And here I thought that maybe you'd found my viral video."

"Nah, I actually hadn't seen that 'til tonight when I googled your name to show my friends your picture so we could figure out why I knew you," she laughed.

The next few days flew by in a blur once we'd gotten settled into a routine of breakfast, practice, games against the other girls who were vying for roster spots. Most of the ladies I'd been on teams with were cool as hell, but this one chick Meredith was just about on my last nerves. She had a chip on her shoulder from the first time we were introduced, which I quickly and correctly read as insecurity because she had been the star pitcher of last year's team but had been shown up by me more than once as we played over the week. It wasn't an intentional thing, but I also did feel a little tingle every time I saw myself gaining an edge on her just because of her nasty attitude. She walked around talking to the other girls with an air of superiority that was full of condescension. She was the oldest person here, five years older than me. There were kids here as young as sixteen with more talent coming out of their pinky fingers than she'd displayed thus far so I'm sure her confidence was shook. That was a personal problem, however. I wasn't here for the childish bullshit.

I was, however, here for today's forthcoming events because my people were coming to town. Tonight, was the first of six exhibition games that we'd be playing against a couple of collegiate level baseball teams from neighboring local universities. We had a three-game stand against our host school's squad this weekend. Pops and Miss Brenda were due to arrive this afternoon with Parker and Blair coming in next weekend. I was excited that they'd get this opportunity to see me back on the mound in real time since I knew that any of them being able to travel internationally was a lark of an idea. And as if he knew I'd just been thinking about him, my phone chimed with a text from my dad. He and Miss Brenda had just landed and were on their way to their hotel. I'd gotten permission from the team's coaching staff for him to be able to come in a little earlier than the rest of the crowd, so I could see him before the game began. I'd be the leadoff pitcher tonight and my dad and I had a little superstitious ritual that we had to complete whenever I'd been given the opportunity to open the game pitching. It dated back to my days of little league and had only been broken during the few games of mine that Pops had missed over the years.

A few hours later, I was standing outside of the stadium waiting for my dad and Miss Brenda to pull up in their rental. It was weird because I was a little anxious, a problem I generally never tended to have before games. Usually, the energy coursing through me was anticipatory, but this time there was a tinge of something else that I couldn't quite pinpoint alongside my anticipation. Soon though, they were pulling up and as soon as I saw my father those nerves completely dissipated. I used restraint and waiting for them to complete their slow stroll toward me instead of running over and launching myself into my Pops' waiting embrace.

"You ready?" Pops said once he was in earshot.

I nodded eagerly, "You brought it?"

He patted the right pocket of the cargo shorts he wore, "Of course I did, Speedy. Let's go."

Miss Brenda just stared on in curiosity as I led the two of them out to the baseball field and my dad and I headed straight for the mound. Once there, he reached down into the dirt, gathering a small portion to smear across the tip of my nose before reaching into his pocket to pull out a fresh pack of Big League Chew. He handed it over to me and I proceeded to rip into it, placing a giant glob of it in my cheek before holding out my hands so that we could complete our secret handshake. Then I spit the gum out into the grass directly behind the mound before high fiving my dad and running to the dugout.

"That...was something," Miss Brenda chuckled when her and Pops had made their way to where I stood next to the dugout.

"It's unmatched," Pops said with a shrug, "Speedy's never lost a game since we created this little ritual."

"No judgement from me," Brenda laughed, "It's actually kinda cute."

"Want me to warm you up a bit, Speedy?" Pops asked, nodding toward the dugout.

I shook my head, "Nah, I don't wanna overdo it. Keni and I were out here a bit earlier.'

"Hey, give us a minute, Bren?" Pops said suddenly, walking over to grab me by the elbow and lead me away from his girlfriend. When we were about ten paces from her when he spoke up again, "Breathe, Speedy."

"I'm good, Pops."

He shook his head. "No, you aren't. It's all in your eyes, Geffri. You're like your mama in that aspect, all of your emotions show on your face. What's going on in your head? Let's talk about it."

"I...I just, want things to go well today, Pops is all. I know that they said I'll be on the roster regardless, but this week has been trying in a couple ways, so I just gotta get outta my head."

"And that Marigold girl needs to get out of your head too."

I laughed, shaking my head, "Meredith, Pops."

"Marigold, Meredith…same shit. You've been given this opportunity because you deserve it, Speedy. Your talent got you here, full stop. Never forget that, kid."

I nodded again, sidling up to him for a hug. "I just want you to be proud of me, Pops."

He wrapped me tightly in his embrace, pressing a kiss to my cheek, "You've already surpassed so many of my expectations for you, Geffri. Have no doubt in your mind that every day you walk this earth you make me prouder than I could ever express. I love you, lil girl."

"I love you too, Pops."

That little moment with my dad pre-game was all I needed to get my mind right. I went into the game with a new mindset, nothing that anyone said to me before I stepped onto the mound penetrated my consciousness. I was completely in the zone and had a helluva game. These kids we were playing against were good, a Division I team that had nearly won a National Championship. I held my own against them though, pitching for six innings and only allowing a handful of them to actually get any hits off of me. When Meredith came in to relieve me at the top of the seventh, however the game completely turned in their favor. We went from having a three-run lead to losing by two when all was said and done. I was pissed, justifiably so since I'd set us up for a good first win, but then she came along and fucked it all up. It was cool though; it was the first game of many and maybe she was just a little rusty despite having been in practice all week. No shade though, I can count on one hand the amount of times I'd seen her really giving her all during bullpen warmups. As we went through the handshake line post-game, a lot of the young guys from the opposing team were giving me props for the heat I'd thrown – a few of them referencing the video from the ballpark that'd gone viral and joked about wanting autographs.

Post-game I had dinner with Pops, Miss Brenda, Keni and her folks. Her people and mine had been sitting together all game so the fathers had built a rapport already and they both had plenty to say about the turn out of the game, particularly Meredith's lackluster performance. Keni had already expressed that she wasn't the biggest fan of Meredith, so it wasn't surprising for me when she joined them in the dragging. I stayed out of it, annoyed but not wanting to dwell on what had happened. We had two more games to get through this weekend and I was more concerned with future outcomes than anything else. I just hoped that the coaching staff would take a look at some of the other girls who could pitch when it came time to construct our lineups going forward. Meredith's ass shouldn't make it out of exposition play, honestly. I'd never seen her game prior to coming here, but from what she had shown so far between me and a few of the youngins we could definitely manage without her bringing us down.

As had become my nightly custom, when Keni and I made it back to the room, I showered, changed into my PJs and took a walk down to the common room at the end of our hallway to call Noah. I don't know why I didn't just take these phone calls in the room because Keni had zero qualms about taking any and every call she received in the room, talking loudly to whoever was on the other end. That was the one drawback to our budding friendship so far, the girl didn't have a modulated volume switch. She was just loud all of the time, which generally didn't bother me because I'd learned to mostly tune it out. Tonight, I'd learned that was a hereditary trait since her folks were just as loud. Since Noah and I were still in the very beginning stage of whatever this was we were doing, it just felt awkward to have the sorts of exploratory conversations in which we often found ourselves embroiled in front of an audience.

"Sup, Speedy," Noah answered when our call connected.

I rolled my eyes. "I should have never told your ass my Pops' nickname for me, now you're just about to abuse it."

"Hey, I got to see how you actually earned that nickname today though."

"How's that?" I asked.

"I saw you steal second on those kids today. You might be the old lady on the team, but you've still got it."

"How did you—wait who are you calling old? You're *older* than me!"

"Yeah, but I have the wisdom of being your elder that would keep me from trying to go out there and keep up with the kids unlike you, babe."

I rolled my eyes, "Oh, I see I've reached *Trollah* tonight. Maybe I should disconnect this call and try to reach *Noah* later."

"Hey! I said you looked good out there, Speedy. Keep that in mind."

"Ugh, shut up!" I laughed, "But seriously, how'd you see the game?"

"Some random Periscoped it on Twitter. Found it when I was randomly scrolling."

"Shout out to technology."

"Right? Wish I could see you in action in person. Soon enough though," Noah said cryptically.

"You keep dropping these hints, but like...you know you can just say whatever it is outright, right?" I teased.

"In due time, Speedy. I know patience isn't your favorite virtue, but practice a little eh?"

"Whateva man," I laughed.

"Nah for real though, how are *you* feeling? I imagine it

had to feel good to get out there and strike out members of one of the best D1 squads. Hell, a couple of those kids are projected to go to the majors, and you were handling them like it was no big deal."

"That's right…gas me, keep it comin'. I need that energy."

"It ain't gas, sweetheart. It's pure fact. You were looking good as hell out there. And I'm not just talking about how those pants be hugging your ass, either. Your arm was like a cannon tonight."

"I can't front. It felt good. It feels good. You know I haven't been playing competitively for a few years now and the energy of the teams I played with were completely different since they were testosterone laden, but this…this feels different and special, but oh so satisfying. I'm just elated for this chance and look forward to seeing what comes of it all when everything shakes out, you know?"

"Okay soundbite!" Noah cracked.

"That did sound a little earnest, huh?"

"I'm messing with you, but I like it for you. I can see it in your eyes that this is bringing you joy, which just makes them sparkle and makes your fine ass *even finer*. I'm happy for you, Geffri."

"Thank you," I murmured, feeling a little self-conscious for some unknown reason. I decided to switch the tone of the convo instead of internally interrogating the feeling. "You ready to be clowned all over the internet in a few days?"

"Oh God. Rai showed me the final cut of the video and I swear…she made it look worse than you beating my ass actually felt. That good ol' movie magic, I guess," Noah chuckled, "I can take the heat about it though. I got the better of the deal in the end anyway."

"Damn right you did."

"Would you find it incredibly weird of me to tell you that I miss being in your presence right now? Because I do."

I said nothing, feeling the heat rise to my face, knowing that I was probably the color of a fully ripened tomato right now.

"Damn, no response. Okay, maybe it was weird. I stand behind it, but I'll keep my thoughts to myself next time," Noah said when my silence lingered for a bit too long.

"Noah," I groaned, "shut up. I'm out of my wheelhouse here, man. We've talked about my previous experience or… lack thereof. Sometimes I just…I don't know what to say in response to the things you say. I just need an extra moment to process, okay?"

"Fair enough," he said, "I tend to just say whatever's on my mind and think about the consequences after the fact."

"Really…woulda never pegged you for that kind of guy!" I teased.

"Here we go," Noah chuckled.

"You can dish and take it, remember?"

"Mmmmhmmm, I remember how *you can take it* too."

I moaned as the timbre of his voice dropped to a more suggestive tone when he continued.

"You need a reminder of how I can give it or nah?"

I didn't know if it was the high of having played my ass off today or the way he bit down on his lower lip as he casually tossed out that inquiry or the shift in his voice, but I found myself biting down on my own lower lip as I nodded in response.

"Nah, sweetheart, I need to hear you say it," Noah crooned.

I shook my head, too embarrassed to speak my desire aloud to for him to do whatever his reminder would entail. He shifted a bit, moving from his slightly reclined position and flipped the phone so that it was pointed directly at his lap, so I got an up close and personal view of the large bulge in the thin basketball shorts he wore.

"Noah, I..." my words trailed off as he put a hand in the waistband of his short and pulled out his dick, "oh my God! Noah, you put that away right now!"

He stroked it once in his hand, "You sure?"

And truthfully, I wasn't sure at all. Not after just seeing the best dick that I'd ever had the pleasure of taking in all of my time on earth. Noah's dick was golden-brown, thick, and beautifully veined. I recalled its heaviness and involuntary shudder wracked my body. Just the sight of it brought the memories of the night we'd spent together and the morning after to the forefront of my mind, unbidden. As he continued running his hand up and down his length, groaning slightly as he increased the pressure, I was rapt and could not help the breathy sigh that escaped my mouth.

"Oh, so that's how it is huh? She's a voyeur not an exhibitionist as I'd initially thought. Okay let me just..." he trailed off before moving once again, switching the camera angle, and propping the phone up on something so that he could get his face in the frame along with his dick that he was still jacking ever so slowly.

"I cannot believe this," I whispered more to myself than Noah, but he chuckled anyway.

"You know what's even more unbelievable," he gritted out.

I shook my head. "What's that?" I panted, completely taken aback at just how turned on I was by what was happening right now.

"That you're getting this show for free. I charge my *OnlyFans* subscribers a lot of money for this premium content," he laughed, before taking his hand off of his dick and tucking it back into his shorts then picking up the phone.

"Hey!" I protested.

"You want the full show, you gotta pay sweetheart. In coins or flesh, the choice is yours."

I rolled my eyes before laughing into a yawn. "Whatever, Noah. I'm getting tired though, talk to you tomorrow?"

"Likely story…I'm wearing you down though."

"Bye, Noah."

"Later, Geffri."

When I got back to the room, the large overhead light was off and Keni's back was to me as she laid in her bed. I assumed she was asleep, so I moved gingerly through the room as to not awaken her. No sooner than I slid into my bed, Keni spoke up.

"You know you don't have to leave the room to talk to your boyfriend, right?"

"I…thought you were asleep. And…he's not my boyfriend."

"Yeah, but I'm saying…this is your space too. You don't have to feel like you can't get fully comfortable here, Geffri."

"That's not it at all, Keni, I promise you. It's just…this thing is new and I'm…lacking a lot of experience so I honestly have no idea what I'm doing most days."

"Caking…that's what you're doing," Keni giggled.

"Whatever! You and Kofi's ass on the phone all hours of the night is caking. I'm just…getting to know Noah. It isn't that deep."

"Yet. Famous last words, ask me how I know."

"How do you know?" I shot back immediately, drawing another laugh out of Keni.

"Because Kof and I were supposed to be friends with benefits and look at where we are now."

"It's way too early to even call something like that between me and Noah."

"I'm just saying. I know I can be a bit much, but I don't want you to feel like any of your personal biz would be compromised if you said something in my presence is all. I'm not like that."

"I know, Key," I said.

"Alright. Now that that's settled...g'nite."

"Night, chica."

The rest of weekend seemed to zoom by since my father was in town. Our Saturday and Sunday games went better than the previous nights did, but still ended in losses. Meredith didn't see any playing time which she expressed like a child might, with a large tantrum in the dugout as the lineup for the game was announced. I had been benched on Saturday as well, but I wasn't fronting. I knew that the purpose of these games was to give everyone a chance to show what they were working with and the thing about me was whether or not I ended up on the mound, I always enjoyed *watching* the game of baseball just as much as I enjoyed playing it. So many people give the game trash for its pace because it is definitely not as quick as most other team sports, but I enjoyed that about it more than anything else. I relished the intensity in a batter's eyes when they stepped up to the plate hoping that they would swing and connect, sending the ball flying as far as possible in order to advance around the bases. The rituals completed as folks stepped up to the plate. The look of determination in the eye of the pitcher to not let the person across from them get the better of them. All of it culminated, for me, in a game that was wrought with a palpable tension that invigorated me.

Things were a little...*weird* the following Monday when we reported for practice though. We hadn't been aware that the team would be halved immediately after that first stint of exhibition games, but I guessed the powers that be weren't playing any games. They knew what they were looking for in a team as well as who seemed to work together best in order to generate the best team chemistry that would eventually lead to us getting some wins under our belt. Thankfully, Meredith's ass was one of the women who were dismissed so

I didn't have to deal with her and that negative ass energy any longer. Keni made the cut and the both of us were super happy that we'd have one another to lean on when it came time to make the trip to Toronto. The intensity of practices had been kicked up this week and we crawled into bed nightly exhausted as hell. I still kept up my nightly calls with Noah, but they were markedly shorter than before. He was busy too, prepping for some major story that would have him traveling for just over a week's time – an exclusive, behind the scenes profile of some player, but he was being super cagey about details when I pressed him.

The thing that kept me pressing on despite this week being brutal was the fact that my girls would be coming in this morning. Our schedules had all been sort of helter skelter, so we hadn't been having our normally, regular group FaceTime chats, so I knew that even though I'd be busy with games, I'd definitely have to find the time to crash in Parker and Blair's hotel room so we could catch up on the happenings in all of our lives over the past few weeks.

"Robinson, can I have a word with you?" Ray asked as Keni and I were walking from the ball field to our dorms.

"Yeah, what's up?" I said, turning back and jogging over in his direction.

"So…we're gonna rest you this weekend, maybe bring you in as a closer for the Saturday game, so that arm is fresh for Toronto," he rushed out on a quick breath.

I nodded, "Okay. Anything else?'

Ray shook his head, "Other than telling you to make sure you bring it when tourney play starts? Nope. I've got nothing. You've been killing it out here. Quiet as kept, a friend of mine told me that you're making waves out here with the clips of you pitching circulating on the internet. Even said there might be some MLB interest. I'm not telling you this with any agenda, but just wanted you to be aware."

"Appreciate the heads up, but I'm just here to play through what's in front of me, Coach. Can't lose time worrying about future possibilities, you know? It's exciting for sure, but I'm not gonna let it distract me."

"Heard," Ray replied, "I like that about you, you know. A major part of the reason that we knew that you'd be an asset to this team is your internal sense of balance. It's one of the first things that we noticed about you after our meeting earlier this summer. You're otherworldly talented, but you don't let it go to your head. The true hallmark of a superstar."

I waved Ray off, "I just do my best and show up trying to win every time is all."

"Aight, Robinson, see you tomorrow."

I nodded once, then ran to catch up with Keni.

"What was that about?" she asked when I caught up to her.

"Nothing super important, just that they're gonna sit me for this weekend's games since they want me to be on my shit for the tourney. You're still coming to dinner with us tomorrow after the game?"

"Absolutely am, but I may duck out on y'all early. Kofi was able to sneak away and will be arriving later sometime tomorrow night."

"Ooh, do you want me to stay with the girls when Kofi gets into town? So y'all can have some alone time?"

"Oh no ma'am – I'm going to lay my ass up in the very expensive hotel room he's reserved and properly reacquaint myself with my fiancé as loudly as I feel like and not have to be ashamed when I have to look folks in the eye the next day."

"All right now," I said, "Don't hurt him."

"Girl, I make no promises."

EIGHTH INNING

"Over here, G!" Blair called out shortly after Keni and I had entered the lobby of the hotel in which they were staying. We were having dinner at the restaurant in their lobby because it was most convenient. She and Parker were currently stationed at the bar situated just outside the restaurant, sipping glasses of wine. We walked over, I made the introductions, the girls had their drink tab shifted to the restaurant and we sat down to dine. Our waiter approached quickly, snagging drink orders for me and Keni before letting us know he'd be back in a few minutes with our drinks and to take the table's food order. Just as I knew it would, the conversation quickly turned to me and Noah, with Blair digging into me less than five minutes after we'd been sat at our table.

"So, how's blogger bae, G?"

I feigned looking at my watch, "Damn fifteen seconds, that's a new record for you, BlairBear!"

Blair opened her mouth to say something smart, I was sure, but then the waiter appeared again with me and Keni's drinks, ready to take our food order. We let him know what we'd like to dine on and then got back into the conversation.

"Obfuscating. That's an old one for you. I already know you been nonstop, long distance caking with the nigga, y'all ain't slick with your little innuendos on Twitter. And chile, we all saw that video from the competition. Anything to win was taken to the next level baby. I thought that man was gonna mount you on the pool table in Smitty's which…if I'm being perfectly honest, would have been kinda hot, G!"

"Blair!" I gasped, fake scandalized.

"I'm just sayin' sis, if there's outtakes of the two of y'alls fine asses on the cutting room floor, I would like to see it."

I lowered my head laughing at her silliness. I could not take it. Noah had taken to publicly messing with me on the timeline, trying to build up some buzz for the video before it actually went live. Of course, when it did go up, not only had he generated buzz among his followers, but that video went viral as well. So, we'd get our jibes off back and forth, mostly Noah coming at me since he was "defending his honor" and of course, me being me, I couldn't let him get too many jokes off, which always resulted in us having little back and forth exchanges. I usually tried to keep it pretty tame, but Noah, *habitual line stepper that he is*, always skirted on the edge of appropriateness and completely absurdity.

"So, spill it, Geff," Parker pressed, "your face is already telling the whole story anyway. It's so cute how you like… actually blush. Swear I didn't think Black girls turned as red as you do when embarrassed."

"Shut up!" I giggled, "It's not that bad. And things with Noah are…good."

"If by good you mean she been laid up caking with the brother for hours on end every night since we've been here, then yep…things are just good," Keni chimed in.

"Oh, we like her," Blair laughed, "We like her a lot, right, PD?"

Parker nodded enthusiastically, "Spill the tea, roomie!"

"All of you get on my nerves," I chided, playfully, "Seriously though, it's wild, y'all. Like, me and dude technically only had one night together but…this feels like it's the start of something great. He's a dope guy and I'm starting to like him a lot. So, we'll see how this progresses. But, enough about me, what about you, Julia Roberts?" I turned to Parker.

"Julia Roberts?" she asked with a confused look on her face.

"You may remember a lovely little film starring one Julia Roberts and Susan Sarandon wherein…" I started but Parker cut me off.

"I cannot stand your ass for this reference," Parker said.

"And that still isn't an answer," I pressed, "So what's tea, sis?"

"Oh, girl she's still over there pining after that man, while hoping their shit progresses like Fran Fine and Mr. Sheffield," Blair broke in.

The entire table burst into laughter.

"On my mama, I cannot stand you either, Blair," Parker snorted.

"What? You know it's true, PDiddy. And I mean like…I can't blame you sis, that nigga is fine. I almost shot my shot at him the other day, but he barely recognized I was in the room. He only had eyes for his future bae."

"Oh my God, it is not like that between us at all, B. We are employer and employee," Parker said.

"I dunno, let's get the opinion of an innocent bystander," Blair replied, turning to Keni, "what do you think innocent bystander?"

"I think that this is none of my business," Keni started.

"Solid assessment," Parker piped up.

"But I also think the lady doth protest too much, sorry Parker," Keni continued and we busted up laughing again.

"Yeah, I definitely like her," Blair said shaking a finger in Keni's direction, "She's my kinda girl."

Conversation was interrupted with the arrival of our food and shortly thereafter, Keni dipped as she got the text she'd been awaiting from Kofi, letting her know that he had landed and was waiting for her. The girls and I ended up wrapping up our dinner and keeping the party going with a couple more glasses of wine at the lobby bar before I bid them adieu and headed back to my room on campus. Since Keni would likely be staying with Kofi for the duration of his time in town, I was going to enjoy having the room to myself. Tonight, I'd get a good night's sleep with the tiny whistling snores of Keni's punctuating the air. Still feeling good off my wine buzz, I took a quick shower and set an alarm to meet the girls for breakfast before their flight in the early afternoon. Before I dozed off, I realized I hadn't heard from Noah at all this evening which was strange given our constant communication over the past couple of weeks. I drifted off into sleep trying not to think too much about it and worrying needlessly.

When I awakened in the morning to no good morning text either, I did get a little worried, so I shot Noah a quick what's up when I was on the way to meet the girls. Got through the entirety of breakfast and seeing them off to the airport with still not a mumbling word from Noah. Still worried, I called him and got no answer. I logged onto Twitter to check his timeline and hadn't seen any content that wasn't auto-tweets of articles pushed from his blog's archives. I tried finding contact info for Jonah or Sarai but came up short. I was a few seconds from emailing the editor in chief of *Atop the Mound* when I got a call from Gretchen asking me to meet her in an all-purpose room on the first level of the dorm in which I was staying. I let her know that I would be right down, curious about what she wanted since she refused to go into detail over the phone. When I got down there, not only was Gretchen in there, but Molly and Ray as well. For a minute I wondered if I'd done something wrong and they were convening this little tribunal to kick my ass off the island. Within seconds I learned that it was the exact opposite.

"So, I can see you're a little nervous about why we called you down here," Gretchen started, "but I promise it's good news. Great news actually. So, Ray told me that he kind of alluded to the press you've been getting the other day and how it's actually doing a lot to raise the profile of the team overall. So much so, in fact, that we'll be having a reporter alongside us for the entirety of the tournament, documenting the team's journey, but mainly – if it's amenable to you – focusing on your contributions to the team and the path that brought you here."

"I...don't know what to say."

Molly chimed in, "We know that you are intensely personal, Geffri, but this is an amazing opportunity to not only shine a light on the emergence of women's baseball as a sport to watch out for, but also for your own personal brand. I'm not sure if you've paid much attention to all the buzz surrounding you, but girl, let me tell you. There are some very important people in very important places speaking your name. This article, if you consent to the angle that this site wants to approach it from, could be the thing that writes your ticket to playing this game on a higher level than you could have ever previously imagined."

"I mean...it does sound like a cool opportunity, but if this article is supposed to be about the team on the whole, why am I the only one being singled out for this chat."

"Well, that's the thing, Geffri, the request came to us for

exclusive access to you for an in-depth profile, not really a piece about the team as a whole."

"Oh."

"And uh…" Ray hedged, "There's one little thing that the ladies have forgotten to tell you. We've kind of already said yes to the article, but under the condition that if you were uncomfortable being the central focus, the writer would broaden it to include the entire team."

"I see," I replied, "Well how long do I have to make up my mind?"

"That's the other thing," Ray continued, "The writer is actually here already. He'll be traveling with us to Toronto and staying the duration of the tournament." He stopped talking to check his phone. "Actually, he just arrived here. We invited him over so you could have a conversation, determine your level of comfort and we could roll from there. If that works for you?"

"I mean, I guess it'll have to work since the guy is already here and all," I laughed, waving my hands, "It's fine. Sure, I'm cool to meet with him now."

"Great, I'll go get him from up front and then you all can have a sit down," Molly said, "Be right back!"

When she left the room Gretchen and Ray were tripping over themselves to assure me that this wasn't something they set up as a publicity stunt. I was taken aback, but honestly it should have been something that I expected. It made sense for whatever outlet to approach the team since I didn't have any representation from a sports standpoint and wasn't exactly seeking the spotlight or to turn this summer of playing ball into much more beyond that. I assured them that I wasn't upset about the situation and we sat in silence until Molly reappeared with the guy who'd be following me around for the next week while I also tried to stay focused enough to contribute to my team winning gold.

EIGHTH INNING · 111

"Ok guys, this is..."

"Noah?" I interrupted.

He grinned, coming further into the room and shaking hands with Gretchen and Ray before easing into the seat next to mine and covertly placing a hand on my knee to give it a squeeze.

"Miss Robinson and I go back a little bit of a ways," Noah said smoothly.

"Oh, that's right! You were the guy in that video on *Atop the Mound* that Geffri completely destroyed," Molly giggled.

"Guilty as charged," Noah said.

"Oh, that makes this all even more perfect. Here I thought we'd have to talk Robinson into letting you trail her this week, but since you all know one another already, she'll probably be more comfortable than we initially thought. Perfect!" Ray breathed. You could hear the relief all in his voice and I fought back a giggle.

"Well," Gretchen said, standing, "I guess we can let you two get to it."

The three of them cleared the room and no sooner than they cleared it, Noah hauled me into him, taking my mouth in a breath-robbing kiss that I was powerless to do anything to melt into. When he'd had his fill, he pulled back, breathing heavily.

"Now that's more like a proper greeting," he grinned.

"How in the world did you pull this off?" I said, my face split by a grin that matched his.

"Told you I'd be seeing your fine ass in person soon," he shrugged, "C'mon, lemme see how you been living the past couple weeks. It's probably better than the extended stay that they got me in for the night until we fly out tomorrow."

Lacing our fingers together, he led me out of the door of the all-purpose room, and we walked up the two flights of stairs to me and Keni's room. When I let him in, he made a beeline for my bed, sprawling across it and patting the scant bit of space beside him for me to make myself comfortable next to him. I strolled slowly, taking my time to come stand near the edge of the bed before he reached out and brought me to lay directly on top of him as he attacked my neck with kisses. I gasped, taken off guard, then giggled when the feather light kisses he'd begun raining down on my neck landed in a particularly ticklish spot just below my ear.

"You have no idea how good you feel right now," Noah growled into my skin, punctuating his words with a suckle to the hollow of my throat, as his hands traversed my back to land on my ass, squeezing and drawing a whimper from me with his movements.

"Aye, Geffri you gotta put a sock on the door if you're gonna be in here playing grabass without warning a sista," Keni called out from where she stood in the door's frame with a hulking figure of a man I assumed was her fiancé standing behind her.

I hopped up off of Noah, blushing and trying to straighten my clothes.

"Hey roomie!" I squeaked, "Noah, this is my roommate Keni and her fiancé Kofi. Keni, Kofi...this is my...Noah."

Noah stood, shaking hands with the both of them who'd now entered the room fully and were on Keni's side of the room.

"We came over so I could pack up and just leave for the airport tomorrow from Kofi's," Keni explained, pulling out her luggage, "Kof also wanted to meet the woman I couldn't shut up bragging on, so...yeah here we are. But I can make it quick so you guys can get back to...you know."

"Oh my God, you're as bad as Blair no wonder the two of you got along so well," I said, before telling Keni about Noah's surprise appearance and the article he'd be writing. I wanted to give her that heads up since she and I spent a lot of time together. And if he was going to be tailing me, then she'd be there for a great majority of the time. Noah assured her that the only inclusion of anything she said would be if she told him the conversations were on the record, but otherwise we should keep hanging and talking as much as usual. Keni packed up fairly quickly and with a hug, she and Kofi were off to make the most of their last night together for a little while.

When we were back alone, Noah just stared at me for a long moment before saying, "So, this was a good surprise?"

I sat down next to him on the bed, burrowing into his side as I nodded, "A great one. Though you almost had me out here calling everyone I knew was tangentially related to you trying to figure out where the hell you were when you went radio silent today."

Noah chuckled, "Yeah, I had to avoid your calls for risk of spilling the beans. I'd been holding this secret for the past week or so, but when I knew it would become a reality, the risk of ruining the surprise went up because I was so damned excited to be able to see you, spend this time, and be given the chance to show the world this amazing woman that I've come to know."

"Flatterer," I deflected.

"Nah, babe, I already told you I'm just a truthteller in the Lord's Army," Noah replied smoothly.

We ended up going out to grab a late lunch and his things from the hotel that he was staying in for the night. It made no sense for him to stay over there when Keni was gone from my room and so we could spend some quality time together alone until we flew out tomorrow. The time we spent together was definitely quality, damn near making us late to meet the larger group at the airport in the morning. If anyone beyond Keni thought anything was amiss with Noah and I arriving in tandem, just barely in time to board the plane to Toronto, they were all smart enough not to say anything aloud.

Since our flights had been booked separately, Noah and I weren't sitting near each other on the way to Toronto, so I used that time to catch up on the sleep that he'd refused to let me get last night. Not that I had any complaints, honestly. The things that he kept me up doing as he maneuvered and manipulated my body to bring me to the height of pleasure? I'd gladly relinquish a year's worth of sleep to consistently feel those passionate feelings of intensity. Upon landing, we took a quick bus ride to the hotel to get settled before a week chock full of action as we played in the tournament. Since he was going to be writing the article, Noah was finally introduced to the team at large on our ride out to the hotel. I saw one of Meredith's little proteges who was still on the team staring a little too long and grinning in Noah's direction, which annoyed me to no end. I let that go as soon as the bus was in motion however, when he slid onto the seat next to mine and gave my hand a quick squeeze before putting enough space between us that could be deemed professional.

When we got to the hotel, however, there was a mishap with Noah's reservation. His employer was to have made sure he was booked at the same hotel as us, but after further review of their communication with our team reps, there was a mix up, placing Noah at a different location of the same hotel brand at which we were staying. Unfortunately, our location was all sold out for the length of time we'd be in town. So, he'd have to be forced to have to commute between his hotel and ours for the duration of our time here since he was still riding on the bus with us to the games daily. A fact that annoyed the hell out of me because I'd planned on tipping out of my room in the evenings and getting in some late-night stretching sessions with Noah. *So much for that, I guess,* I thought bitterly as he got in an Uber to roll over to his hotel and check in. When he made it there, he wasted no time FaceTiming me trying to convince me to sneak out of mine and come see him, but the day of travel got the best of me and I demurred.

Our first game was not slated until midday, so Noah called me bright and early, convincing me to dip out of the team's breakfast and do a little exploring with him. He wouldn't tell me what we were going to do, just that we would be back to my hotel in time to get on the bus. I honestly didn't need much convincing to spend time with him, so I easily acquiesced, begging Keni to give an excuse if anyone asked about me when she met up with the rest of the team to eat. I dressed casually, in a cute little sundress and flat sandals and left my hair down in its wild naturally wavy state since Noah had hinted more than once that he was a fan of my "lion's mane" as he referred to it. When I stepped out of the hotel, Noah was standing there looking entirely too good with the sun hitting his golden-brown skin. He was dressed in a black tee-shirt that molded to his perfectly formed biceps and cargo camo shorts.

"Good morning, gorgeous," he crooned, dropping a quick kiss to my lips before leading me to an idling taxi. "Our time is money today, babe, so we gotta get a move on."

"You still don't wanna tell me where we're going?" I asked, sliding into the car before he did.

He shook his head. "Trust me though, you'll love it."

I said nothing more, taking in the sites of the city as we maneuvered the streets to our destination and when we finally came to a stop, I looked over at Noah curiously.

"Are we going up in there?" I said, pointing to a large building – one of the world's tallest – made even more famous by its appearance on a Drake album cover. "Because now would be the perfect time to inform you about my extreme fear of heights."

"That is not our destination, but that information is filed away for any future excursions we may take. We're actually going in there," he said pointing behind me, across the street.

"Excuse me?" I asked, trying to keep the excitement out of my voice once I'd turned to view the building he pointed toward.

He nodded. "I pulled some strings and was able to snag us a little private tour action. You up for it?"

"You bet I am," I said, lacing our fingers together and dragging him toward the Rogers Centre. "How in the hell did you pull this off?"

"Well...I remembered in one of our conversations you mentioned your fascination with one of the Blue Jays' most hallowed pitchers and his journey, so I made a call to a man who made a call to another group of men and were able to pull this off. Thought it would be cool to let you spend a little time on the mound over here before you headed out to pitch your own amazing game."

"Wait...you said a tour. We..." I tried tamping down my excitement. "We've got field access?!"

He nodded once slowly before looking down at my feet. "I guess I shoulda given you a heads up about footwear, huh?"

"Meh, it's not like I haven't gotten a little dirt on me before," I grinned.

Noah let us to a side entrance where we were met by a Blue Jays' representative who gave us the two-cent tour of the arena before leading us down through the dugouts and onto the field. Noah and the Blue Jays rep lagged behind a little bit as I made a straight beeline to the mound. I stood there, briefly closing my eyes and taking in a deep breath. In the far recesses of my mind, I could hear the roar of a crowd as they cheered their home team on to victory. In this little fantasy, the game was dependent on me and one last pitch to seal our win. I wound up and let one fly – hearing the imaginary crowd in my mind grow louder as the pitcher swung and miss.

Noah walked up slowly, chuckling, "Game winning pitch was a strike?"

With no shame I turned to him grinning, "Did you doubt it would be?"

He kept moving forward, pulling me into a loose embrace. "Not for one minute, sweetheart," he replied before leaning down and placing a kiss on my lips that quickly turned from the innocent peck that I was sure he intended to a torrential lip lock.

"Thank you," I said when we pulled apart, "for this. This is pretty cool."

"I'm glad you approve. Thought it might be kinda lame since you've been on a professional mound and dazzled thousands before."

I shook my head. "But I've never been on a mound on which one of my top twenty pitchers let 'em fly. This is *beyond cool* for that reason alone. Thank you…for bringing me here, making this happen."

He tried waving me off like this was no big deal, but I knew it to be the exact opposite. Whoever he got to pull some strings probably had him on the hook for any number of favors now. We stood there silently for a few minutes more before Noah nudged me along. He insisted that we needed to get a move on to get some breakfast in me before my big first day of the tourney. I honestly was a bit too nervous and excited to actually consume an entire meal, but I let him drag me to a quick breakfast before we needed to get back to the hotel to roll out with the rest of the team to the field. While we were at breakfast, I'd received a text from Parker and Blair wishing me luck on today's game. Pops had also called, and I spoke to him briefly as we were in a car back to the hotel so I could change. I was kind of sad that he wouldn't be here today, but I knew that I needed to make sure that I did my very best, making him proud from afar.

The ride from the hotel to the ballpark we'd be playing at was unusually quiet. Noah and I passed a bit of the time answering some of the questions that he'd had for me for his article, but the fact that most of the other girls were in their own worlds not really interacting with each other had me feeling a way. After about ten minutes I'd had enough and stood up trying to get everyone's attention.

"Ayo!" I called out a few times until all eyes were on me.

"What is this energy brewing around here? Because it seems a little too timid for me right now. We're about to play our first game of this tourney and I don't know about y'all but I'm excited. We've got a bomb ass squad; these girls can't see us out here. But y'all all slumped like we about to be sent up for the slaughter." I shook my head defiantly. "Hell nah, I don't like that energy. Key, where's that little Bluetooth speaker you be having? Give us some mood music for the rest of this ride."

Keni immediately got into gear, getting some music going in a manner of seconds. I danced down the main aisle of the bus, engaging everyone – either making them get up and dance or at least acknowledge me with a fist bump, high five, *something* if dance wasn't their ministry. Within a couple minutes, I'd changed the team's energy and by the time we pulled into the parking lot for the ballpark we were on a high, singing along with the music playing at the top of our lungs and having a good ass time. I made my way back up to Noah whose face was covered with a look of admiration. Pretty soon he was just as wrapped up as the rest of us, chanting and singing along with the music playing.

We carried that energy from the bus onto the field, handily winning our first game in the tournament with a score of nine to two. Not only had I pitched amazingly, I'd

EIGHTH INNING • 119

also had a helluva day at bat – with two ribbies and a triple that eventually ended in me scoring a run. Despite buzzing off the high of winning, I felt a bit down when I couldn't get in contact with my dad post-game. On the rare occasion that he was unable to make any of my games, he was always the first person I spoke with once the game was over. I didn't want to pout about it, knowing he'd call me when he saw the missed call, but I still felt a little sad. I tried not to let it show on the ride back, but Noah could tell that something was bugging me. He tried asking about what was going on, but I didn't want to talk about it. All I wanted to do was get back to my hotel room, take a long, hot shower and rest up for the following day's game. And when we got back to the hotel that's exactly what I exited the bus to do. I brushed off Noah's overtures to get me to come back with him to his room and walked inside.

I'd gotten three steps toward the elevator when I heard, "Chin up, Speedy! You just played an amazing game."

I looked up to see my father and Miss Brenda standing right near the elevators. I couldn't help my excitement as I ran full speed at him, launching myself into his waiting arms and burrowing my face into his neck.

"You really thought I wasn't gonna come see my best girl playing at the biggest stage of her career?" he asked, gruffly, but I could hear the tightness of his voice nearly cracking with emotion.

"I'm so glad you're here, Daddy!" I sniffled as I pulled back.

"Wouldn't have missed it for the world, kid, you know that!"

I hugged him again, a little tighter before pulling back and hugging Miss Brenda too. They told me that they would be staying for the entirety of the tournament because the expectation was that we'd make it all the way to the championship match. Pops suggested that I go rest for a bit then meet him and Miss Brenda in the lobby so we could all go to dinner later.

"You can invite your little friend, too," Pops said as we got onto the elevator.

"Keni? Oh sure, I'll let her know when I get up to the room."

"Nah," Pops shook his head, "the young man, what's his name, Noah?"

"I...he...we're...not at the meet the parents stage, Pops."

"Nothing wrong with a friendly dinner, right? Besides, you said he was writing an article about you right? Well that won't be complete without my two cents, so...make sure he knows he's welcome to join us for dinner tonight."

That sounded more like an imperative than a request so I just replied, "As soon as you guys make a reservation, let me know so I can let him know."

"Sounds good, see you in a few hours."

Dinner ended up going surprisingly well, with Pops and Noah hitting it off immediately. Hell, they talked more to each other than anyone else at the table once it came out how much of a Negro Leagues enthusiast Noah was. He and Pops ignored the rest of us in favor of talking about baseball history as me, Miss Brenda, and Keni talked about everything but baseball – both Keni and me wanting to think about anything but the game that employed us currently. Plus, I knew that despite being with my dad baseball wasn't really Miss Brenda's thing so I wanted to create a conversation that would be inclusive. Somehow, we ended up on the topic of TV shows and she gave me a gang of suggestions to binge on Netflix. She had a little addiction to television and it definitely showed because once we got her going Miss Brenda couldn't shut up about her shows. She even pulled out her phone to show us a little calendar app she had to keep track of all the shows she watched in real time and via DVR.

The night ended with Pops' and Noah exchanging contact information like I didn't exist. I mean, I wasn't quite beat to be their messenger, but I also didn't know how I felt with Noah and Pops bonding so quickly when he and I were still in the beginning stages of whatever this was we were doing. That was probably the last thing that should have been on my mind at this point in time, but it still bugged me a little. I didn't say anything though, just blushed a little too hard when Noah wrapped me in an embrace that lingered a bit too long before he hopped into his Uber going one way and we hopped into ours going the opposite way. After Pops and Miss Brenda got off the elevator at their floor once we reached the hotel, Pops doubled back, sliding a hand in the double doors to catch them before closing.

"By the way Speedy, I like that young man for you. He's got a good head on his shoulders."

Flummoxed by Pops' words, I said nothing in return, just nodded my head and endured the teasing from a merciless Keni as we rode to our floor. I couldn't stop the grin from spreading on my face as Pops' assessment sank in though. Because the more I got to know him, I liked Noah for me too.

NINTH INNING

This week had flown by and despite a couple hiccups, we were currently the only undefeated team in the tourney, standing at the top of the leaderboard. It was an amazing feeling and I should have had no worries since the team that stood between us and the gold was the very first team that we'd handily beat. However, this morning I woke up with an uneasy feeling that I couldn't shake. Instead of grabbing breakfast with Noah, my Pops, Miss Brenda, and Keni, I stayed in the hotel room, hoping that maybe just a little alone time was what I needed to shake this funk. That wasn't the cure as I was on the team bus, trying to keep up the façade of being hype like everyone else, but deep down I was freaking out.

Last night Ray had pulled me aside, praising me for my all-around success during this tourney and I knew he meant well, but something in his little speech was a trigger. I was notoriously hard on myself when it came to achievement, a big part of why I'd deigned to no longer participate in organized sports after undergrad. The only reason why I was here now was because I knew that this was something that

Pops had dreamed for me and I couldn't stand to let him down. And it'd been fun, no pressure or anything – just going out night after night, doing my best and contributing to the team effort. Being singled out for excellence always caused me to put undue pressure and stress on myself which ultimately led to me being…where I was currently – plagued by doubts of whether or not I could really pull this off.

Now, as I was warming up in the bullpen before the game began, I was trying to shake the nerves. I knew that we could do this. The ladies had been playing with sort of a feverish desire to win at all costs. We were out there raking – ladies who'd rarely hit doubles, bringing in homers. Our defensive reflexes were catlike, no woman getting past us without a tag out if it was within our power. The shit was just…unlike anything I'd ever experienced before. Our chemistry was kinetic. Now was not the time for me to be doubting them, let alone myself. I tried shaking it off but carried whatever this feeling was with me into the game. After four innings and giving up three runs, Ray signaled for a timeout.

Trotting off the mound and over to the dugout with the rest of the team, my head was low as I tried to shake off whatever these sudden nerves were. No sooner than I'd cleared the field, Ray started in on me asking if he needed to let one of the younger, yet more experienced players take the mound since I couldn't seem to pull it together and I didn't even say anything to try to convince him that I needed to stay out there. If he felt a changeup was necessary, who was I to protest? Keni immediately spoke up.

"All due respect, Coach? What we ain't finna do is that. We wouldn't even be here if it wasn't for Gef. No diss to anyone else here because we're all capable players, but G is the heart and soul of this team. She gets our spirits going and keeps the momentum up when everyone else is dragging, but we haven't been keeping that same damn energy with her.

This entire tourney, she's carried the team's morale on her back," Keni said before turning to the rest of the ladies, "But now maybe it's time for us to give her a little of that energy back, yeah? If you need an inning or two to get your mind right G, that's cool. But we don't win without you on that mound when it's all said and done."

"Well?" Ray huffed, with an attitude I couldn't completely fault him for, but still made me a bit on edge.

"I need a minute. Izzy, you ready?" I asked another pitcher who'd been our alternate starting pitcher.

"Born," she grinned.

"Bet," I nodded, "Coach, I'm sorry for…whatever this is."

He waved me off gruffly. "Daitey is right. Do whatever you need to, but your ass better be ready to close this thing out."

Despite him putting on the angry man façade, I could tell that he was really thrown by my behavior and hell I was too. Before I knew it, I'd made my way back to the locker rooms, digging through my stuff to find my phone to see if I could get Pops to make his way down here. I could really use some of his energy. I shot a group text to him and Noah both – because I knew it would be difficult for Pops to gain access down here but knew that with Noah's credentials it'd make the process somewhat easier. I sat there for what seemed like hours but in actuality was only about ten minutes before I saw Pops' smiling face peeking around the corner.

"Really, Speedy? This again…" Pops said, shaking his head at me, "And this is why you should have brought your ass to breakfast, lil girl. C'mere."

I wasted no time rising and running straight into his arms. He said nothing, just held me as I released a few shuddering breaths before speaking.

"What if it all goes to shit again, Pops?" I asked.

Sitting there waiting for him to arrive, I realized what had me so shook. It was my senior year of high school all over again. I'd been fairly well known around my home state, namely because a girl playing baseball was a novelty so whenever I did the smallest thing, the biggest deal was made of it. So, when I assumed the position of our starting pitcher and my arm led us to the state championship, and then promptly let us down by letting my nerves get the best of me? It was a bit of a rough time. I went from being a shutout pitcher to letting some guys who should have never gotten a single off of me send balls flying to the far most reaches of the outfield. That loss was tough, with the opposing team's final run coming via a changeup pitch that I'd thrown that was read by the batter almost immediately and he knocked that motherfucker clear across stateliness. It'd taken me years to get over it, something Pops teased me about mercilessly once I was truly over it.

"Then it goes to shit, baby girl. That doesn't change the impact that you've had on this game...this tournament...*hell, USA Women's Baseball on the whole*. You have been excellent, Geffri. Perfect? Not by a long shot, but you've kept your cool in some tough situations this week and you've managed to prevail each and every time. That isn't by luck. It's with skill that you've carefully honed. The power lies within your hands, baby girl. And I know you've got it.," he said, pulling back and placing his hands on my shoulders while looking me straight in the eyes, "*you* know you've got it. Now is time to show and prove. Let's go, kid."

And with that he walked out of the locker room without a backwards glance. A second later, Noah was peering into the locker room.

"You good?" he asked, moving tentatively as if he was expecting someone to kick him out of here.

I nodded, not trusting my voice after Pops' impassioned

speech. Everything he said was the truth, but I couldn't seem to shake the nervous feeling in the pit of my stomach.

"You sure?" Noah asked again when he was close enough to wrap me in a loose embrace with his arms looped around my waist, "Because you don't look like it."

"I just…it's silly," I said, shaking my head, "I'll be all right."

I tried pulling out of his embrace to head back toward the field, but Noah held onto me tighter.

"Nah. See, I wasn't trying to be all in the Kool-Aid, but Mr. Leon's voice travels, so I heard a lil bit of y'alls conversation and…he's right, baby. You *are* excellent. And you know what?"

I shook my head no because I had no idea where this was going.

"Y'all will win and you'll pitch the final out. And then I'll be able to tell everybody that my girl is a gold medal winning baseball pitcher and hear them tease me mercilessly for my days of being a sports hero being far behind me."

I giggled at his silliness before he covered my mouth with his, drawing me into a quick but potent kiss. Pulling back slightly, but keeping his arms around my waist, Noah asked, "You ready to go back out there?"

I took a deep breath to gather my bearings then nodded my head. "Yeah. I need to get back out there."

"Aight, superstar. See you at your medal ceremony," Noah winked before strolling off.

I took a few moments more to myself before heading back onto the field. I was about halfway back when something occurred to me…had Noah referred to me as *his girl*? As in homegirl…girlfriend…I wasn't quite sure, but the last thing I'd needed was another thing to stress about, so I filed that away as something to discuss with him later. When I got back to the dugout, Ray remarked that I looked a helluva lot better than I had when I left and sent me to the bullpen to warm my arm up again. At the next possible chance, he relieved Izzy from the mound and I took my rightful place. We had two innings left and we were up six runs to the three I'd given up earlier.

As we passed, I whispered to Izabella, "Way to hold 'em!"

"Bring home the gold, Gef!" she replied with the same level of enthusiasm.

I nodded in return. All I needed was six outs and we'd walk away champions. A simple feat, but that didn't change the feeling of the weight of the world on my shoulders when I took the mound. I took my time getting settled, eyes searching out the crowd to find Pops whose eyes were squarely on mine as he mouthed "you got this!" The first three outs came easily and in the bottom of the inning I had an at-bat where I batted in two runs to increase our lead going into the ninth. I was feeling better than good, knowing that only three outs stood between me and a championship—something I'd been fighting for in all of my years of competitive sports, but had yet to achieve as player. The nervous tingles from before morphed into anticipatory excitement.

The last three batters were among the few who'd actually gotten hits off of me earlier in the game and I couldn't front like I wasn't still feeling the nerves when the first girl came up to bat. But once I got her out of here easily in three simple strikes, my confidence skyrocketed. The next batter got a base hit, but the one after her went down easily as well. With one person on base, two outs, and their best batter coming up to the plate, I could feel my heart pounding quickly in my chest. I took a moment, shaking my arms out, cracking my neck from side to side before I got into my stance to throw my first pitch. I peered over to Keni who briefly flashed three then two fingers, signaling for me to throw an inside curveball. I shook my head at her, remembering the last time this chick was up she hit damn near a homer off me with that same first pitch – an inside curve.

Instead, I threw a four-seam fastball, gauging how quick she would be to jump on a pitch. She went for it, missing far and wide which only served to bolster my confidence. Keni signaled for me to repeat the pitch, which I did gratefully. This time old girl came closer to getting a piece of it, but barely connected, so now we were at two strikes. I took a second before setting up to throw the final pitch, taking in the moment with the crowd, despite not being a home crowd, cheering intensely for us to bring home this win. As the sound swelled, I dug deep to tune it all out, becoming one with the ball as I let my final pitch fly – a changeup this time since I knew she expected the fast ball and I wanted to lull her into a false sense of security. She bit, swinging with quite a bit of power behind it, but missing the ball completely. I saw but couldn't hear the ump call that third strike as my entire team stormed the mound. Keni was the first one to make it to me, throwing her catcher mask somewhere behind her as she grasped me to jump up and down in jubilation at our win. I was so damned shocked that I'd actually managed to pull it off that I was frozen, in the moment but not fully conscious of it. I didn't snap back to reality until some jackass decided to douse the team with the large Gatorade jug that'd been in our dugout.

As the cold liquid ran down my face, I felt it commingling with tears of which I hadn't been previously aware. We'd really fucking done it. *I'd really fucking done it.* All of the post-game press, the medal ceremony…all went by in a blur for me. I was still sort of in disbelief that we'd actually won the whole damned thing. As soon as I saw my Pops though, my haze was broken. I ran to him – Gatorade soaked and all, throwing myself in his arms. I damn near knocked the both of us over, but he steadied us quickly.

"You did it, Speedy. I told you," he whispered, his voice cracking with emotion, "I'm proud of you, kid."

"Thanks, Pops," I said, thickly trying to tamp down a fresh round of tears.

"Howsit feel?"

"Surreal...honestly. It hasn't really sunk in, you know?"

"You gotta be in the moment, Speed. Remember every part of this, catalog every emotion, so you can tell your kids one day what it felt like to be on the rise to the absolute peak of your career."

"You don't think this is it? Winning a gold medal isn't the peak?"

Pops shook his head, "Nah, you still have so much more to accomplish, Speedy. The best is yet to come. Let's get outta here and continue celebrating. Bren and ya lil boyfriend over there looking left out."

I looked over my shoulder, behind us where Noah and Miss Brenda stood, both with different looks of anticipation on their faces. I laughed at Pops' commentary before leading him over to where they were standing, accepting first Miss Brenda's then Noah's embraces.

"Proud of you, *Speedy*," Noah teased as he wrapped his arms tightly around me, pressing a brief kiss to my cheek, "I'll have to wait until we get back to a hotel to show you exactly how proud though. Wouldn't want Mr. Leon to put hands on me outchea."

I blushed, giggling while shaking my head, "You are a mess."

"A mess that's gonna convince you to spend the night with him instead of listening to the Keni symphony?

I bit my lip, looking up at him as if I needed time to contemplate.

"Don't try to front on me girl, you know you ready for this congratulations all over your body."

We both were silent for a beat before bursting into laughter.

"How about I forget you said that?" I cracked.

"Please do. The sooner the better," Noah replied sheepishly.

After showering back at the hotel, followed by a quick nap, I packed up my things to head out to Noah's for the night.

"Shoulda known…" Keni teased as I gathered my toiletries from the bathroom, "Gon' head and get to ya man. Just make sure y'all make it to the airport on time this time."

I shook my head. I couldn't do anything but laugh. "I dunno, Key. I make no promises."

"That's my girl," she said, rising from where she'd been fake napping to come sit on my bed.

"Been a helluva week, huh, kid?"

"Helluva *few weeks!*" she replied exuberantly, "But honestly, I'm so glad that you were here with me through them. I…don't make friends easily, most folks think I'm too loud or too bold or too brash, but I've spent way too much time toning myself down for the sake of others, you know? Felt good to be wholeheartedly embraced while just being myself. So, thank you, for that."

I came around from the side of the bed I was on packing to wrap her in a strong embrace. "Damnit, Key, don't get me to crying up in here! For real though, you're amazing and authentic and a friend for life, sis. Hell, Blair might ditch me for you at any moment. This ain't the end. Because I'm fully expecting my invite to you and Kofi's wedding *and your bachelorette festivities.*"

Keni giggled, "You and your plus one are fa sho invited."

Just then my phone went off.

"Speaking of your plus one," Keni teased while handing

me the phone that was closer to her as it was charging on the nightstand between our beds.

It was a text from Noah wondering what was taking me so long. Shortly thereafter another text came through and I was so glad that I had turned off message preview because the last thing I needed Keni to see was the picture that accompanied that message. I quickly wrapped up our good-byes and got my ass in the elevator down to the lobby so I could call a Lyft to Noah's hotel to let the real celebrating begin. Halfway through my descent, the elevator stopped on my father's floor and I prayed that it wouldn't be him and Miss Brenda getting on the elevator. Jesus was not my homeboy on this day, however because that was absolutely who was stepping onto the car.

"You taking off already, Speedy? Thought your flight wasn't until tomorrow like the rest of us," Pops said.

"I..."

"Leave her alone, Leon. Enjoy your night, sweetie. We'll see you back home," Miss Brenda cut in.

Totally grateful me was really a half a second from telling Pops to gon head and put a ring on it.

"Aw Bren, she knows I'm just teasing," Pops laughed.

The ding of the elevator letting us know it reached the ground floor was a welcomed intrusion as I rushed from the elevator, dragging my bag, with a parting greeting yelled over my shoulder. My Lyft arrived quickly, and we were at Noah's hotel in no time. Thankfully he'd slipped me his spare key earlier, so I let myself into the room. I walked in to see him just as he'd been attired in the photo he sent. Body clad in nothing but snug, black boxer briefs, with a cocky grin stretched across his face. I was barely two steps into the room before he was on me, kissing me with pent-up passion as if our last time together wasn't in the very recent past.

He stripped me bare, donned a condom and was inside of

me in no time flat, but I had zero complaints. Not one complaint at all as he slow stroked me, whispering words of a congratulatory nature in my ear. And when he snaked a hand between us, strumming my clit with barely there swipes of this thumb, my legs began to shake as my cries for release grew louder and louder. I came in a quivering mass of wetness, gasping as Noah kept going, driving into me with powerful strokes through his own release. He collapsed onto me, but I welcomed the comfortable weight of his body pressed against mine and cried out in protest when he slid to my side, pulling me into him in a loose, spooning hold.

"Was that a fitting enough celebration for a champ," he rasped into my ear.

"Absolutely," I grinned, turning in his embrace to press a quick kiss to his lips.

We laid there in silence for a few minutes before I spoke up again.

"Hey," I said, gnawing on my lower lip, "so you said something earlier…and I…I just wanted to get clarification on something. Not trying to back you into a corner or anything, but I was just…curious. When you said 'my girl' earlier, did you mean like…"

He cut me off, silencing me with a kiss before I could even get the rest of my question out, "I meant like, *mine*. No one else's. And *not* just my friend. Is that cool with you?"

I nodded. Yeah, that was *definitely* cool with me.

POST GAME INTERVIEW

Noah

After spending more than a few minutes with Geffri Robinson, it's evident that she has three major loves of her life - her family, her friends, and baseball; in that order. That pecking order is most evident that when you ask about her baseball origin story. Her eyes grow soft with affection as she details the special relationship she and her father maintained as he raised her as a single parent. Baseball was an integral part of the glue that held them together through the years – first with her father taking her the games from the tender age of two onward and later with him being a supplemental coach as she decided to take on the sport on her own.

"Pops is...God, if it wasn't for him, none of you all would know my name," she says with conviction, "He is the reason why I am who and what I am. If it wasn't for him...my love of the game, the care and precision that I take when I'm on the mound? Sorry to those skills, they wouldn't know me if I walked up to them on the street." She paused to giggle at her little joke. "And they're all byproducts of being Leon Robinson's baby girl." Mr. Robinson,

when asked about the role he's played in his daughter's success is far more modest. "Speedy [his nickname for Geffri] has always had this innate specialness. I saw it in her even if she didn't see it in herself. All I ever tried to do was encourage her to pursue it."

Her journey so far definitely details that specialness – numerous high school accolades, including still holding the record for the pitcher with the most wins, a storied undergraduate career that most were sure would lead her straight to making strides to be the first woman in the MLB, but somewhere along the way the fire of that goal was snuffed out. Robinson doesn't go into detail when pressed about what made her put down her glove after her collegiate years; instead choosing to switch gears to talk about how her new team has ignited an even stronger fire in her than before. She goes down the line from the program director down to each individual teammate—citing positive attributes of every single person involved with the Team USA Women's Baseball organization. Once again, showing that uniquely coded spark of specialness that pervades her spirit. When asked by her teammates to describe her in one word, the two repeated most often were tough and kind. Two words that are typically at odds, but when deployed in tandem are key ingredients to the recipe of a great leader.

I sat back from the keyboard, trying to come up with the perfect way to continue summarizing Geffri as a player and person in fifteen hundred words or less when the woman in question wandered into my office, clad only in one of my tees with her hair splayed about her shoulders in a mess resembling a lion's mane.

"Are you working?" she asked in her silky, sleep-roughened voice that I was certain she didn't even realize was a turn on.

I waited until she was within arm's reach to snake an arm

out, dragging her onto my lap and burying my face in her neck to murmur, "Not anymore."

She giggled before pulling back, "I thought you were on deadline. Let me not interrupt your flow." She tried escaping my clutches, but I was stronger.

"Nah, I'm just about finished. Wanna read it?"

She shook her head furiously, "Absolutely not. I still can't believe it wasn't a huge conflict of interest for you to even write this darn thing especially considering that we're...you know..."

"We're what? I wanna hear you say it, babe."

She blushed, just a little before speaking. "Since we're together. Dating. Boo'd up. All of that."

"Which honestly makes even more sense for me to be the one writing this, gorgeous. What other sportswriter at *Atop the Mound* has seen you at your absolute best and worst? I'm giving this piece depth after plummeting your depths. Wow, your man is talented out here, baby."

She rolled her eyes. "He's also super humble."

"Yeah, but you love that shit though. It's how I got you."

"Oh please, I decided to let myself have you, there was no *gotting* to be done."

"So, you're saying if I didn't slide in your DMs..."

"I still woulda bagged you, eventually. Once I decided that I had to have you. It's just that simple. Look at my track record – if I believe it, I achieve it," she replied cockily.

And I let her have it because honestly there was no use arguing about who took down whom because we both got the better of the deal. These past few weeks since we'd been home from Canada were filled with nonstop caking when she wasn't busy with all of her teacher related things. After her performance in that international tournament, there had been rumblings of some MLB teams having interest, but Geffri hadn't paid any of the conjecture any mind. Her mindset was until she got a call, there was nothing to get riled up about. It was honestly one of the things that I really liked learning about her the closer we grew, her easygoing nature. She wasn't easily ruffled and operated with an air of confidence that was off the charts sexy.

"You *had* to have me, huh?" I replied, cockiness all through my tone, "Let's get back to that."

She nodded, biting her lip and moving in closer to whisper in my ear, "And I'll take you now, if you're offering."

I rose up from my office chair, as Geffri yelped, wrapping her legs around my waist and steadying herself in my embrace. I quickly strode from my office back to my bedroom, none too gently depositing her onto my bed and hovering atop her.

"Say less, sweetheart. Say less."

Afterword

If you enjoyed this book, please consider leaving a review on Amazon and/or Goodreads.
Keep up with my podcast #FallsonLove at:
www.nicolefalls.com
Follow me on Twitter:
www.twitter.com/_nicolefalls
Follow me on Instagram:
http://www.instagram.com/_nicolefalls
Like me on Facebook:
https://www.facebook.com/AuthorNicoleFalls
Join my Facebook Group:
https://www.facebook.com/groups/NicsNook/

About the Author

Nicole Falls is a contemporary Black romance writer who firmly believes in the power of Black love stories being told. She's also a ceramic mug and lapel pin enthusiast who cannot function without her wireless Beats constantly blaring music. When Nicole isn't writing, she spends her time singing off key to her Tidal and/or Spotify playlists while drinking coffee and/or cocktails! She currently resides in the suburbs of Chicago.

Also by Nicole Falls

Accidentally in Love Series:
Adore You

Smitten

Then Came You

Holliday Sisters Series:
Noelle the First

Brave Hearts

Started From A Selfie

The Illumination of Ginger

More to life series

Someone seeking someone else

Nymphs and trojans Series (collaboration with Alexandra warren)

Shots not taken

Lessons in love series (collaboration with Bailey west and Té russ)

Road to Love

Distinguished Gentleman Series (anthology collection organized by book euphoria)

Switched at Bid

Standalone Titles

Sparks Fly

Last First Kiss

SUGAR BUTTER FLOUR LOVE

ALL I WANT FOR CHRISTMAS

A NATURAL TRANSITION

F*CK AND FALL IN LOVE

Made in the USA
Middletown, DE
02 February 2025